Praise f

"Michael Rowe's talent shines through in this terrifying story of social persecution, black magic, and desire gone horrifically wrong. Readers will immediately identify with the story of Mikey Childress, and they'll hold on for dear life as Mikey's search for acceptance and a dream of love drag them across a jagged terrain of brutality and indifference. With *October*, Rowe taps into the primal terrors of a teen's life, exploring the loneliness and misery of an outcast who finds his only salvation in a vicious, dark place."

—Lee Thomas, Lambda Literary Award, and Bram Stoker Award-winning author of *The German* and *Down on Your Knees*

"*October* is the kind of horror novel a lot of adults needed when they were kids. Michael Rowe understands that while it gets better for some people, not everyone can afford to sit back and wait if they want to survive. A powerful and powerfully frightening tale about making hard choices in the name of survival, and what those choices cost. Because becoming who you are really means making a deal with the Devil. And sometimes, the Devil is the only one who really understands."

—Bracken MacLeod, author of *Stranded* and *13 Views of the Suicide Woods*

Praise for October

MICHAEL ROWE
OCTOBER
A NOVEL

FIRST EDITION

October © 2019 by Michael Rowe
Cover art © 2019 by Erik Mohr (Made By Emblem)
Interior & Cover design © 2019 by Jared Shapiro

Distributed in Canada by
Fitzhenry & Whiteside Limited
195 Allstate Parkway
Markham, Ontario L3R 4T8
Phone: (905) 477-9700
e-mail: bookinfo@fitzhenry.ca

Distributed in the U.S. by
Consortium Book Sales & Distribution
34 Thirteenth Avenue, NE, Suite 101
Minneapolis, MN 55413
Phone: (612) 746-2600
e-mail: sales.orders@cbsd.com

Library and Archives Canada Cataloguing in Publication

Title: October / Michael Rowe.
Names: Rowe, Michael, 1962- author.
Description: Reprint. Originally published: Peterborough: ChiZine Publications, 2017.
Identifiers: Canadiana 20190104430 | ISBN 9781771485012 (softcover) | ISBN 9781771485296 (hardcover)
Classification: LCC PS8635.O884 O28 2019 | DDC C813/.6-dc23

CHIZINE PUBLICATIONS
Peterborough, Canada
www.chizinepub.com
info@chizinepub.com

Edited by Brett Savory
Copyedited and proofread by Sandra Kasturi

Canada Council   Conseil des arts
for the Arts   du Canada

We acknowledge the support of the Canada Council for the Arts which last year invested $20.1 million in writing and publishing throughout Canada.

ONTARIO ARTS COUNCIL
CONSEIL DES ARTS DE L'ONTARIO
an Ontario government agency
un organisme du gouvernement de l'Ontario

Published with the generous assistance of the Ontario Arts Council.

Printed in Canada

OCTOBER

"There are spirits that are created for vengeance,
and in their fury they lay on grievous torments."
—Ecclesiastes 39.33

For John Larson

And in memory of John Sumakis,
aka David Thomas Lord

August

July

June

May

April

March

February

I would die for love, Mikey Childress thought, as he lay on his bed in the airless heat of his bedroom. *Yes, I would die for it.*

Sweat made his black Misfits t-shirt cleave to his skinny torso like a second skin. Mikey rolled over on his stomach and buried his face in his pillow, closing his eyes. In the red darkness there he called forth a familiar waking dream. He contemplated love. Not sex necessarily, just love. Just not being alone. That would be the key.

Mikey conjured the sense of a warm body spooning into him, his narrow shoulders pressed against a stronger, larger upper chest, of arms encircling him from behind. They would be the sort of arms that could throw a football in a perfect arc, the sort of arms that hang insolently out the driver's-side window of a car—sinewy biceps and thick, capable forearms that ended in hands that were rough from sports, strong and capable and authoritative. He imagined his lower back and ass pressing into a solid pelvic basin and the hungry, pressing swell of desire he would find there. He called forth a pair of powerful legs, one of which would be thrown possessively over his own thigh, pulling him into the fully conjured body he now imagined claiming him with an irrevocable desire he didn't want to resist, even if he could resist.

He ground his pelvis into the mattress of his confining single bed, finding familiar comfort in the sensation of pressure against his groin.

What could be sweeter?

Mikey sighed as he imagined laying his head gently against the base of the phantom's hard clavicle. He dared to imagine the solid knob of an Adam's apple against the back of his head. The dream-arms pulled him in closer, making him feel as weightless as an autumn leaf. He sighed again, holding the sorcery of the moment, knowing it would vanish the instant he opened his eyes and let in the cruel light. He closed his eyes tightly, summoning the incubus with all his might. With the intensity of a prayer, or a spell, he willed the invisible to become visible, gave it flesh and muscle and heat. And love. Endless, everlasting love.

Someone to love me, someone to hold me, someone to protect me. Someone to be all mine. Yes, I would die for it. If I met the witches tonight, I'd tell them I would kill for love.

In August, in a small town, there is still peace for a teenage outcast like Mikey Childress.

An outcast can still choose his companions in August and is, for the most part, subject only to his own demands. He can make his own hours. Hell would begin again in a few short weeks when school resumed. At that time he would again be subject to schedules not of his making and companions not of his choosing, and the daily dread that had to be endured beyond the point of being endurable.

The town of Auburn dozed at the foot of the cliffs and ravines of the Niagara Escarpment under the heavy August sky like a stout country dowager in a rocking chair, one who had gathered the rich southern Ontario farmland around her like a quilt in order to ward off an imaginary chill. Wedged between Milton and Campbellville, Auburn thought of itself as a self-contained universe and was smugly proud of what it considered its separate identity. It had a population of 3,200 souls, and few of them would want to live anywhere else. Main Street ran the length of the downtown core, such as it was, and was lined with shops, the post office, the library, the town hall, and the offices of the local paper, the *Auburn Gazette*.

In the residential section near downtown, the streets were wide and deep, the houses set back from the road on good-sized lots under an arching cathedral of poplar, elm, and maple trees. Most of the houses dated from the nineteenth century and were done in the classic southern-Ontario style of muted red brick with white gingerbread trim. The lawns were well-tended, the walkways bordered with shrubs and flowerbeds. In the summer, the somnolent green haze carried on it the sound of lawnmowers and the scent of fresh-cut grass and flowers, In autumn, people in Auburn still burned leaves in the backyard while the town constable looked the other way, and the smoke drifted generally, mingling with the scent of ripe apples and chilling dark-earth harvest from the farmers' fields outside of town.

It was a town that prided itself on its rectitude. Able-bodied men worked and provided for their families. Those women who didn't stay home with their children worked in town and were considered unfortunate. There were four churches in Auburn—the Catholic St. Benedict's, the Anglican St. Michael's, and the Lutheran St. Martin's. The fourth, the Assembly of Christ's Holy Stripes, was a rogue fundamentalist sect founded by an ex-con and self-proclaimed "pastor" named Kelvin Cowell. The Holy Stripers, as the assembly was referred to in town, met in a converted industrial warehouse on the outskirts of Auburn for three-hour services Wednesday nights and Sunday mornings, and their brand of Christianity was harsh and pitiless.

Mikey had lived in Auburn his entire life and felt he could account for every bruising minute of those seventeen years. He knew there was a world beyond the town because he'd read about it in books and magazines and on the Internet. He'd seen that world on television and in the movies as well. He knew it was a clean place, one where people like him didn't get beaten up nearly every day at school, or after school when the bullies, who roamed like packs of callow teenage jackals, had a freer range of territory in which to hunt him and more time to plan how best to torture him with the least chance of getting caught.

In the world beyond Auburn, people like Mikey didn't get slammed into lockers nearly every day until purple contusions bloomed on their chests and upper arms like pulpy grapes. They didn't get their heads forced into toilets that were then flushed, producing a terrifying sensation of drowning as the victim took in water and shit when he screamed—only to be pulled up brutally by the hair at the last minute, coughing and sputtering, to the sound of coarse, brutal adolescent male laughter. On good days it didn't happen twice, and on great days the toilet was flushed before the dunking.

By and large, there were two places where Mikey felt safe: in his bedroom and in his head.

His room was a walled fortress where he could be himself. His books were there—wall-to-wall bookcases full of paperback horror novels and books on demonology and witchcraft, some dating back to the 1950s and before. His passion for the supernatural was something that isolated him even further from his peers. If he had lived in another time and place, he would have known that an interest in horror fiction and horror movies was a time-honoured, and honourable, nerd trope, and all he would have needed was one friend with whom to share it. Auburn, however, was a hockey town. If you were a boy, you played sports. The overlapping circles of exclusion fanned outward from that core premise. He had his horror novels and his books on the occult, and he had his computer.

His mother had begun attending the Assembly of the Holy Stripes church three years before. Although a certain intuitive levelness kept Donna Childress from crossing the line that divided the yearning, questing soul in search of arbitrary boundaries in a world gone socially fluid from the true-blue fanatic, her conversion had become a source of enormous friction between herself and Mikey's more or less agnostic father. Larry Childress thought Kelvin Cowell was a fraud and a crook. When Donna had come home one Wednesday night in tears after Cowell had lectured her on the dangers of "being yoked to an unbeliever"—to wit, her husband—Larry had threatened to drive over to the church and break Cowell's legs. What ensued proved to be one of the worst fights of their marriage. Larry tried to forbid Donna from attending the church, but she refused. As a compromise, she agreed to tone down her religious rhetoric around the house. It was an uneasy détente, broken only once: the time Donna tried to throw out Mikey's books on the occult, and his computer. Although Larry Childress neither liked nor approved of Mikey's fascination with horror fiction and witchcraft, he was unwilling to cede any more ground to his wife's religious obsessions. It was one of the few times Mikey could remember that his father had intervened on his behalf against his mother's wishes.

In any case, they agreed on other things about him. As disappointed as his parents might have been about what they perceived as their only child's effeminacy and isolation from the world of his peers—and, in Donna's case, the source of fearful, unasked questions about her son's sexual orientation and its potential effect on whether or not they would eat the Bread of Life together in heaven or not—it had fortunately not occurred to either of his parents that their son's computer and Internet access were providing him with yet another refuge from the crushing brutality of the world in which both of them seemed to thrive. It was a world, after all, that they themselves had traversed with stolid, unremarkable aplomb in their own day.

The Internet was Mikey's window to the outside world, and a mirror of sorts against which he measured Auburn based on a series of assets and liabilities that always had the town coming up short. Someday, he thought, he would leave Auburn, or run away, or escape by means legitimate or otherwise.

The town wasn't without a special history that appealed to Mikey's esoteric fascinations. Auburn and, to a lesser degree, Milton and Campbellville were possessed of an unusual number of legends of the sort that are kept alive primarily by word of mouth from generation to generation of the town's youth. Mikey knew them all by heart. Occasionally the stories would be tied to individual people, none of whom, of course, were still living in the town—or even living. This made them harder to completely disavow than, say, the more generic urban legends that thrived elsewhere and which had been packaged and resold to the populace by Hollywood in any number of slasher films.

Auburn and Milton prided themselves on their own organic folklore. An urban anthropologist might have been interested in the fact that this tiny obscure tract of southern Ontario farmland, bordered by the hard granite cliffs and chasms of the Niagara Escarpment, could lay claim to its very own indigenous aggregation of dark fables—a commune of werewolves living in the hills, for instance, or vampires, or trolls, or a coven of witches—but that would presuppose that any urban anthropologist would ever even hear the stories. The townspeople of Auburn and Milton kept their devils to themselves the same way they kept everything else to themselves. But Mikey, like all the young people in town, had grown up with the stories. He had even found a couple of sites online that mentioned sightings of the witch coven, but beyond that the stories stayed within town limits.

Over in Milton—on Martin Street, for instance—was the red brick Victorian where old Mrs. Winfield had lived during the first half of the twentieth century. Her husband had vanished sometime during the 1920s. Although she was rumoured to have killed and eaten him, those were just stories. In the early 1970s, an eleven-year-old boy named Randy Murphy was found in her cellar on Halloween night. He had survived an attack by a wanted child predator after trick-or-treating, but the story he told about how he'd wound up in Mrs. Winfield's cellar—and about Mrs. Winfield herself—was much, much worse. The police ascribed his story of vast underground rooms beneath her house to shock, but when Mrs. Winfield moved away shortly after, the town released a collective sigh it hadn't realized it was suppressing.

In the 1980s, the house had been purchased by two men who kept to themselves. One of them was allegedly a writer, a strange fellow who only came out a night and seemed eager to make friends with the locals. His "gentleman friend," as the Miltonians referred to his companion, was rumoured to be a musician of some kind. He, likewise, was only ever seen after sundown and, even then, rarely. One stormy winter night, a seventeen-year-old boy named Vinnie Mancini, a cook at a local restaurant where the so-called writer often dined, vanished from Milton along with a redheaded waitress named Juicy.

After three nights, his hysterical mother began receiving phone calls late at night, purportedly from Vinnie, telling her that he had run away with Juicy. The police were unable to do much beyond listing him as a runaway since, by his mother's own account, he had called her and told her so, though she had begged him to investigate "those two faggots in that house on Martin Street," one of whom had been the object of her son's curiosity on the occasions that he'd come into the restaurant. While the police were sympathetic to Mrs. Mancini's plight (and privately didn't disagree with her characterization of them as "faggots"), they had been unable to establish a link between them and Vinnie's disappearance. Over time, the two men came to be thought of as victims of small-town prejudice, gossip, and a mother driven mad with grief. They eventually sold their house and slipped away from Milton one night like mist.

The following year, when Vinnie turned eighteen (it was assumed he had turned eighteen, and was alive and living somewhere), he even lost the designation of "runaway." But until his mother died two years later—diagnosis: pernicious anemia—she told everyone who would listen about the dead sound of Vinnie's voice on the telephone when he called her in the hours before dawn and told her about his new life, and about the nights she dreamed she saw his pale, hungry face floating in the darkness outside her window, his fingernails scratching the glass as he entreated her to let him in from the cold.

There were tales of a commune of outlaw bikers who lived somewhere above Glen Eden on a sprawling, derelict farm and, at night, under the full moon, they cast off their human form and became wolves. Again, people had seen the bikers occasionally when they came into town for provisions, but no one knew anyone who had seen them actually *shapeshift*. There were no such things as werewolves, though it made a great story late at night.

There were the stories of the coven of witches—*real* witches, nasty ones, like out of fairy tales, not what the townspeople referred to as "white-light tree-huggers"—who purportedly performed obscene rites beneath the full moon, rituals of blood and sacrifice and dark magic. Over the last fifty years there had been numerous alleged sightings in remote fields, usually by teenagers who had been out late, or drunks wandering home from a night of revelry. Of all the town's legends, these were the most persistent. For that reason they were given a little more credence by the very same people who would have scoffed at stories of vampires and werewolves and trolls.

Of course, if they existed, they weren't *real* witches, but then again, the town worthies said, these days it only seemed to matter what you thought you were. Anyone could call himself or herself a "witch," but it only made them a hippie, or a nutcase.

Mikey told himself that Wroxy Miller was his best friend, though, truth be told, she was his only friend, and he, hers. Essentially friendless—she by choice, he by circumstance—neither dared skirt the edge of the question of whether or not each would have given the time of day to the other if either of them had been cool. It was safer not to ask. They told each other that they were rebels and held to the pact. Besides, their love for each other, even forged as it was by circumstance, was genuine.

They had met on their first day at Auburn High School, in grade nine, three years before.

That day had begun as a secondary-school version of Mikey's entire scholastic career. The same boys who had tormented him in junior high were back, only they seemed to have acquired a new viciousness over the summer as androgenic hormones and testosterone accelerated a new, combative intensity. Twinned with this warrior-like perspective was a raging new awareness of the opposite sex. Like young male animals, the boys now considered the competitive stakes much higher when it came to attracting girls, and knowing what to do with them once you'd caught one. This in turn seemed to necessitate reminding "that little pansy freak" Mikey Childress of his place in the social order of the pack.

Karol Verbinski—called Dewey by anyone who wished to survive their interaction with him—had started lifting weights during the summer, and he told anyone who would listen that he intended to become a bodybuilder.

Jim Fields, his best friend, had decided that if Dewey was going to be a bodybuilder, so was he.

They had both put on bulk and sinew during the summer. During a weekend away in Kitchener, where they'd stayed with Dewey's cousin, Vanya, Jim had received his first tattoo. It had earned him a weeklong grounding, but his parents couldn't watch him all the time.

Furthermore, Jim thought, as he flexed his triceps in the bathroom mirror after his shower at night, it looked fucking cool.

Behind their backs the other kids called Jim Dewey's "shadow" and laughed about how they two of them shared one steroid-addled brain between them.

Dewey was short and bull-necked, one of those boys who seemed to grow muscle as a birthright. He wore his hair cropped short and had worked all summer at the warehouse in Milton where his father was a foreman. It wasn't legal to hire minors for that sort of work, but the owner of the warehouse trusted and admired Dewey's father, and was content to turn a blind eye while Verbinski's tough little fireplug of a son hauled boxes and was paid out of the petty cash so his father could teach him a work ethic.

Dewey's parents, Stash and Yalda, were old-country Polish Catholics who spoke very ungrammatical, heavily accented English. This was something that Dewey was more sensitive about than he ever admitted. At eleven he had beaten a boy named Johnny Treleaven so badly for parodying his father's thick Slavic accent that Johnny had wound up in Milton District Hospital with a mild concussion and two broken ribs.

When Johnny's parents, Joan and Walter Treleaven, had insisted that charges be laid against Dewey, Johnny had become hysterical and begged them not to go to the police.

Fearful for his life (literally, for Dewey had two large, barbarous older brothers), Johnny told his parents that he had started it, and that it wasn't Dewey's fault. When Joan insisted, Johnny had grown so frantic that the nurses in the hospital came running in and demanded that his mother leave. The subject was never raised again after that, and Johnny would eventually be transferred to a private school in nearby Oakville.

Stash had forced Dewey to apologize to Johnny at the hospital. Johnny sat up stiffly with his back pressed against the headboard, as though trying to break through the rear wall to get away from Dewey, who mumbled that he was sorry. When Dewey extended his hand to Johnny, the boy flinched.

"I think it's time for my son to rest," Joan Treleaven said with glacial courtesy. "Please take your son home, Mr. Verbinski. This sort of hooliganism may be commonplace where you people are from, but this is *Canada*"—she leaned forward, enunciating each syllable of the word as though speaking to someone who didn't understand English at all—"and I assure you, in this country, it is not."

"My son Karol was born here, Mrs. Treleaven," Stash said, stung. "I been here twenty years. I work hard, I teach my son. I'm sorry that he have done this. I ask you to forgive me."

"Goodbye, Mr. Verbinski. My husband and I would prefer it if neither of you came back while my son is in this hospital. If you do, I will inform the police and ask them to see to it that . . . *Karol* stays away from Johnny. And we *will* press charges."

White-faced with shame, Stash Verbinski had backed out of the hospital, mumbling a litany of apologies in broken English while Joan Treleaven looked on impassively. He grabbed Dewey's arm roughly and shoved him into the corridor. Later, at home, Stash punished Dewey with a savagery he had never before shown his son. While Yalda watched and wept, Stash pulled the eleven-year-old's pants down and whipped him hard with a thick leather belt until Dewey was screaming in pain. Broad red welts rose on his legs and buttocks. The more Dewey pleaded that he had only beaten up Johnny Treleaven because he had mocked Stash's accent, the angrier Stash became and the harder he whipped him. He stopped only when he broke the skin of Dewey's upper thigh and saw his son's blood.

Privately, Stash wished he could be whipping Johnny Treleaven instead. He was deeply embarrassed by his bad English and hated the idea of being the object of Johnny Treleaven's derision, but he had the immigrant's fierce pride when it came to making a life in the new country. This included fitting in and getting along with his new countrymen.

That said, though Stash would never admit it even to Yalda, his son's capacity for rage and violence frightened him, and he was determined to rein it in with strict discipline. The irony of his methods didn't occur to Stash, who was of another age and culture. Dewey never forgot the beating, and he never forgave his father for it. He also never forgave Johnny Treleaven, whom he blamed for the rift between himself and his father, whom he loved still.

As the years passed, though Dewey wasn't aware of it in any sentient way, his hatred for Johnny developed into a generalized, slow-simmering fury toward anyone he perceived as more vulnerable than he himself had felt under his father's belt. Dewey never broke anyone else's bones, or put anyone in the hospital, but he grew mean and sullen as his adolescence unfolded. Despising weakness in any form, Dewey built up his body with an old weight set his brother, Andrea, had picked up at a garage sale years before, and publicly proclaimed that the thing he hated more than anything else was "faggots." In the clumsy, brutish argot of adolescent boys who had never met a homosexual, or even considered the concept of homosexuality, Dewey meant the word as a catchall for everything feminine and sensitive, and therefore undesirable, in a male.

Though he had never contemplated whether Mikey Childress was indeed, specifically, a homosexual, he considered him a prime, grade-A example of *faggotry* in every sense of the word.

While Mikey was terrified of Dewey, as were most of his peers with any survival instinct at all, at thirteen he harboured a secret, all-consuming crush on Jim Fields.

Jim was a laconic jock, not too bright, with a slow, lazy smile. Girls had discovered him in the sixth grade, and the attention hadn't let up. Jim was tall and lean, with broad shoulders and thick black hair. His eyes were antifreeze blue. To Mikey he looked like Joshua in *The Ten Commandments,* a movie his mother watched several times a year. Donna was always delighted when Mikey joined her in front of the VCR for "The Ten Cs," as she called it. She saw it as a hopeful sign that the Lord was working inside her son, to turn his mind and soul toward more hopeful things. For his part, Mikey had memorized every scene that included a bare-chested Israelite slave or Egyptian soldier, and secretly imagined himself as Lilia, the water girl played by Debra Paget, with Jim Fields as John Derek's Joshua.

Mikey wrote love poetry about Jim in the privacy of his bedroom after school and drew hearts in the margins of his notebooks with *J* and *M* intertwined inside. He never saw a teenage couple holding hands in the hallway at school or strolling through the Milton Mall without a bitter awareness that he was alone. Every girl he saw was himself, every boy was Jim Fields. Occasionally Mikey wondered how he could envy them their happiness, and find them beautiful, while at the same time realizing that their happiness would never be his.

It was still the first week of high school when Mikey first met Wroxy, the same day his chief nightmare, Dewey Verbinski, tripped him in the lunch line at the Auburn High School cafeteria. Even as he felt the horrible lurch in his chest as his body arched in midair when his foot flew out from under him and he pitched toward the greasy floor of the lunchroom, he wasn't shocked. The random, public cruelty of this particular act had become so much a part of his life that Mikey expected it. His knapsack fell off his shoulder, spilling out the contents. A well-worn copy of Clive Barker's *Weaveworld* that Mikey had saved up for fell—pages out—into a filthy puddle of half-dried tapioca pudding and spilled milk. His new portable CD player went skidding across the laminated concrete floor toward the opposite wall until Jim Fields stopped it with a short kick. Mikey saw that he was wearing his scuffed black engineer boots, the ones with the square toe and the side buckle above the anklebone.

Jim cocked his head to the side, the way a beautiful, intelligent dog might, and stared at Mikey benignly. His full mouth curled into a smile that seemed to Mikey almost loving. For a suspended instant Mikey locked eyes with Jim, and he was sure that Jim would reach down in one graceful, gallant, athletic movement and hand Mikey the CD player, then help him up. Jim would explain that the tripping had been a mistake and apologize for his fucktard no-neck friend, Dewey.

In the cluster of seconds it took for this glorious fantasy to ripple across the surface of Mikey's imagination, Jim gracefully raised his booted foot and brought the heel down as hard as he could, smashing the CD player into shards of broken plastic and twisted wire.

The sharp crack ricocheted off the walls like a gunshot, and the lunchroom exploded into terrible, dark laughter. They laughed and laughed, till the walls echoed, as though the sight of that pathetic loser, Mikey Childress, red-faced and crying—for by now, Mikey was sobbing, his heart as broken as the CD player—was the most hilarious thing they had ever seen. Whether anyone's mirth was leavened with relief that, at least this time, they weren't themselves on the receiving end of Dewey's and Jim's cruelty was something no one would admit, much less at that moment.

"Whoops," Jim said mildly, his smile broadening as Mikey's face twisted in pain. "You shouldn't leave your shit lying around, faggot. It can break."

More laughter. Jim was rewarded for his loyalty with a backslap from Dewey as Mikey fled the lunchroom. The last thing he saw as he dared a half-turn toward the hot-food counter was Jim and Dewey collapsed against each other, laughing till tears streamed from their eyes. Even in a moment of such abject wretchedness, Mikey remembered to walk, not run, as though there was any dignity left to salvage, lest he seem so beaten as to invite further derision or, even more monstrously, a reprimand from one of the staff for running in the halls.

Escaping into the bright September sunshine, Mikey, weeping, sat down on a bench near the far side of the playground and wondered how to kill himself with the least amount of pain. He discounted hanging. He could swim, so drowning himself in the waters of the Glen Eden gorge was out of the question. Likewise, he didn't have a gun, and his mother didn't use sleeping pills.

Mikey heard the doors at the entrance to the school slam open. He looked up and saw a girl dressed all in black coming toward him, scuffing along with a curiously defiant gait. She wore burgundy Doc Martens, and her hair was cut in a Mohawk. As she came closer, Mikey saw a nose ring glint gold in the sun against her pallid skin. She carried a large black velvet bag that seemed packed full of books—mostly horror novels, Mikey noted, spotting the new Anne Rice hardcover and a couple of paperbacks by Stephen King and Douglas Clegg—and CDs. The sight of the horror novels in her bag, all of which he owned and had read more than once, surprised him. He was usually derided by his peers and teachers for reading what they called "trash," and his mother, who had more or less given up on trying to turn him into anything like a "normal" boy, in her words, never shied away from her view that his infatuation with horror fiction wasn't healthy and would eventually lead him over to "the dark side," away from God.

As the girl walked toward Mikey he looked up into her face. He had noticed her sitting at the back of his class earlier in the day, head down. She'd spoken to no one that he could tell, but Mikey, as usual, had been more interested in not attracting attention to himself than in noticing new arrivals. He'd heard some of the girls a couple of desks ahead of him whispering that she was some dirty slut who had just moved to Auburn from "the city," that euphemism for everything Babylonian and foreign from the uncharted region down Highway 401, past the safe borders of Milton, Auburn, and Campbellville. And now here she was, walking toward him. Her head wasn't down anymore.

She looked him straight in the eye and said neutrally, "You'd better stop that crying. If you don't, that shit will never stop with those assholes. You have to get tougher." She paused and cocked her head in a way that wasn't dissimilar from the way Jim Fields had done moments before he'd smashed Mikey's CD player. In the girl's face, however, Mikey saw only compassion and genuine concern. "Trust me, I know. Are you okay, dude?"

Mikey, who had never been called *dude* in his life, gaped up at her and said, "Yeah, I guess so. How about you?"

"*Me*?" The girl laughed. "I didn't just get kicked onto the ground by a no-neck jock and his butt-buddy who broke my CD player. Yeah," she said. "I'm okay. It's you I'm worried about, dude."

She extended her hand. Mikey saw that the nails were short and painted black. He took her hand and shook it.

"I'm Wroxy—that's with a *w*," she said. "I've just moved to this shitty little redneck town from Vancouver. My parents just split up and my whore of a mother decided to move back to her hometown with me. My father didn't seem to care too much, so here I am in fucking *Auburn*." She spit on the ground. "Not even *Toronto*, which would have been bad enough, but here I am with Bill and Mary Six-Pack and their inbred hairyback children in the middle of fucking *nowhere*." Wroxy let loose another string of stunning profanity.

Mikey smiled in spite of himself, then began to laugh. Accustomed as he was to being made to feel like the freak at the bottom of every social pyramid since grade school, he found the notion intoxicating that this absurd-looking but impossibly sophisticated girl from Vancouver was deriding those he had been taught to think of as his betters.

"What's your name, dude?"

"Mikey," he said. "Mikey Childress."

"Well, Mikey Childress," Wroxy said, fishing inside her enormous velvet bag, "this is your lucky day."

"It is?"

"Yes, it is." She withdrew a brand-new Sony Sports Discman from her bag. It was bright yellow with a hard plastic shell. In her hand it looked as incongruous as a canary coming from the black velvet folds. She handed him the Discman. "Here," she said. "Take it. My dad gave it to me before I left Vancouver. Can you believe the colour? Fucking *yellow*. Uh, not me. As if my father even thought before he bought it."

Mikey gaped. "For me?" He reached for it, then hesitated. She couldn't possibly mean that she was giving it to him. "You're *giving* me your Discman?"

Wroxy said wryly, "Well, it isn't as if you have one currently. This one won't break the next time that hunchback trips you, or if that fucking Ken doll with the black hair steps on it. Who were those two anyway, and why do they hate you?"

"You can't give me this. You don't even know me." He guiltily ignored her pointed question about Dewey and Jim. It seemed to him as though this stranger's act of kindness might have been extended under a misapprehension on her part, and might be withdrawn if she realized how pathetic he was. "Besides, what will you use? You can't just give this to me."

She said sweetly, "Oh, I have another one at home. A *black* one. *Much* more me. I got it at a stereo shop in Toronto last weekend." Wroxy smiled slyly and winked. "Five-finger discount, dontcha know.

"You stole it?" Mikey was indignant. "You stole it from a *store*?" He had never stolen anything.

Wroxy shrugged, looking bored. She handed him the brilliant yellow Discman. "You want this one, dude? No strings, no bullshit. I didn't steal this one. It's from my dad, honest. And if you want it, it's yours. You seem like you've had a pretty shitty morning. Seriously," she said softly. "I know what it's like."

Mikey looked earnestly into Wroxy's face as wordless communication passed between them.

When he was convinced that there was no malicious punch line waiting, no hidden laughing chorus, no barbed guile, Mikey took the CD player from Wroxy. It was still warm from her touch. Their fingers brushed lightly as she handed it to him.

"Thanks," he said. "That's really nice of you."

Wroxy drawled, "Whatever." She looked sideways at Mikey and half-smiled. "I have a question for you. It might be kind of a weird one, so please bear with me, okay?"

"What?" Mikey turned the Discman over in his hands, marvelling at the bright singing yellow of it, and how pretty it was.

"What about the witches in this town? Ever heard of them?"

Mikey looked up. Backlit, her face was briefly in shadow, her brilliant black crescent of a Mohawk like a noonday eclipse. He squinted into the sunlight.

"The witches?" he said dumbly. "How do you know about the witches? You're not even from here."

"Oh, please," Wroxy said, sounding bored. "Anyone who knows about this supernatural shit has heard about your mysterious coven of witches out here in Auburn. It makes sense, with all your fucking churches on every corner, that there would be something to counterbalance it. The universe is like that," she added loftily. "Do you know what that means?"

"I may be a loser but I'm not stupid," Mikey said. "I know what *counterbalance* is. You know," he said testily, "just because you're from Vancouver doesn't make you better than the people who live here." Even as he said it, Mikey wondered why he was defending the Auburnites who had given him nothing but grief and pain for as long as he could remember.

"Actually, it does," Wroxy said. "Small-minded hicks are the worst kind of people on the planet. They tend to be bigots, they never travel, they think everyone else is like them, and they're obsessed with religion. There are, like, four churches in Auburn. Do you know how many bars there are here? One. There's one bar and four churches. Fucking hicks, I'm telling you."

"I'm surprised you're willing to talk to *me* then. Me being a hick and all."

"I didn't say *you* were a hick. I said the people who *live* here are hicks."

"*I* live here," he snapped. "In case you haven't noticed."

"I bet you wouldn't live here if you didn't have to, though, right?"

Mikey was silent. She had him on that one, that's for sure.

"Now, what about those witches? Have you ever seen them?"

"No, I haven't," he said. "I don't know anyone who has. I mean, people have said they've seen them, but I think it's more like an urban legend, personally. Well, except that Auburn isn't exactly what you'd call *urban*."

Wroxy looked despondent. "No," she said. "That's for sure. Man, I miss home." She brightened. "Hey, if I tell you something, will you keep it a secret?"

"I guess. What?"

"'I guess' isn't the answer I was looking for, dude. Can you keep it a secret or not?"

"You haven't *told* me anything yet," he said, beginning to enjoy bantering with the girl. It was something of a novelty. "How can I keep something secret that you haven't told me?"

"Swear!"

Mikey smiled. "All right. I swear. What?"

"I'm a witch," Wroxy said proudly. "You know. Like, I have powers. I can make things happen. I can cast spells and shit."

Mikey stared at her blankly. Wroxy fumbled inside her black jacket and withdrew a large pentacle on a gold chain. She brought it closer so that Mikey could inspect it more closely. He peered at it, then pulled away.

"You know, around here you could get beaten up for wearing something like that to school," he said. "They call that kind of stuff Satan worship around here."

"Witches don't believe in Satan. In the craft, there's only energy. It comes from the earth, and from the god and the goddess."

"Well, in Auburn that'll get you into trouble. But yeah, I won't tell anyone, okay?"

"You do believe me, don't you?" Her voice was hopeful. "That I'm a witch?"

To Mikey she sounded a little worried, as though it actually mattered to her what he thought of her. He was momentarily confused, then stunned to realize that Wroxy actually seemed to be making overtures toward a bond of friendship. For some reason this strange new girl wanted him to like her. For the first time, he saw something beneath her bluster that brought her closer to earth, made her seem more of the sort of girl who might perhaps have some insight into what it was like to be Mikey Childress 24/7.

"Yeah, I believe you," Mikey said gently. "I believe that you're a witch. And no, I won't tell anyone. I swear."

"Does that freak you out? You know, that I'm into this stuff?"

Mikey mutely offered her his knapsack. Wroxy reached inside and pulled out *Weaveworld*. She opened the book and frowned when she saw the page that had been damaged when it had fallen onto the floor of the lunchroom. With a light touch, she smoothed the page and closed the book, replacing it in Mikey's knapsack. She handed the knapsack back to him, and another moment of recognition passed between them.

"Barker rocks," she said approvingly. "*Weaveworld* is one of my all-time favourites of his. It's not really horror, but it has some awesome moments that are scary as hell. Like the scene of that angel coming back to life or whatever and burning up everything in its path as it tries to get at the hero. Totally awesome. I love his stuff. And *Hellraiser* is my all-time favourite movie of his. I love horror fiction." Her eyes were shining. "It's all I read, basically."

"Me, too," Mikey said. "Pretty much nothing else. I don't know anyone here who's like that."

"Poor baby. Try being a girl reading horror fiction. We're all supposed to be reading *Sweet Valley High* or some such shit."

"These people think horror is sick or something."

"*These people*," Wroxy said, "are, basically, cattle. If any of them had an original thought, they'd make sure it was okay with their friends first." She stood up. "Come on, dude." She gathered up her black bag and turned to look at Mikey. "We have to get back inside. The bell will be ringing for class any second, and we don't want to get you in any more trouble than you already are." She extended her hand. "You can sit next to me if you want."

"Hey," he said, curious in spite of himself. "Can you cast a spell on Dewey Verbinski? Can you make him look like a troll or something?"

"Dude," Wroxy said dryly. "If you mean the guy who tripped you, it looks like someone beat me to it." She giggled. Her hand was still extended. Mikey hesitated, then took it.

That was the beginning of a friendship that was literally life-sustaining, at least to Mikey.

Of course, Mikey soon told Wroxy about the witches of Auburn, and all the other stories as well.

Then, three inseparable years passed, and it was August.

6

Wroxy had been christened Roxanne, a name she had detested
from childhood. She'd gone from Roxie to Wroxy six years ago
when she was ten and still living in Vancouver. In an act of stunning self-actualization and prescience, she had remade herself,
deciding that since her peers hated her anyway, she was going to
be the most dramatic-looking pariah at any school she attended,
ever.

"They look like boiled beef," Wroxy had told Mikey contemptuously during the first winter of their friendship. She'd surveyed
the lunchroom crowd from the vantage point of the farthest table
as they filed past the hot food counter. "How did Scotch-Irish
people get to be so stuck up about their origins? Look at those
girls—big asses, red faces, blue eyes. Ugh. Spare me. And that's
just the girls. Don't get me started on the guys." Wroxy shivered
delicately and took another sip of her Diet Coke.

"Isn't your mom Scottish? I could have sworn she was."

"My mother's family is *Welsh*, originally. *Big* difference. The
Welsh are known for their mysticism and their awareness of the
spirit world. Stevie Nicks is Welsh, you know. That's what the song
'Rhiannon' is about."

"Stevie who?" Mikey had known full well who Stevie Nicks was. He had lip-synched enough Fleetwood Mac songs in the privacy of his bedroom to not only know but imitate her perfectly: arms akimbo, flipping his imaginary hair in time to his snapping hips, his woolen winter scarves flying like Stevie's silk ones in the videos.

"Never mind," Wroxy had snapped. "You're hopeless."

Often Mikey told Wroxy that she looked a little like Winona Ryder in *Beetlejuice*, a generous exaggeration on Mikey's part that Wroxy took with a grain of salt when she contemplated her doughy, shapeless body in the mirror every morning as she dressed in her uniform of all black. Her skin was pale, usually clear and lovely, something Wroxy's mother always pointed out to her when she was bewailing Wroxy's spikey, dyed-black hair, or her weight, or her Goth clothes.

"That's what they tell all us fat girls, you know," Wroxy said one Saturday afternoon as Mikey watched her apply her shoplifted MAC makeup in the mirror of her basement bedroom, which was painted blood red.

"You're not fat," Mikey had said with reflexive loyalty.

"Yes I am," Wroxy had replied. She shrugged. "I don't give a fuck."

"What do they tell them?" Mikey was fascinated by makeup. He loved watching Wroxy apply it. Wroxy layered her foundation and powder thickly in a shade that went beyond ivory and into the realm of white. She smudged black eyeliner and shadow around her blue eyes, then painted her lips deep purple. Mikey thought she looked beautiful.

"They tell them, 'Oh you have such pretty *skin!*' Or, 'Oh, you have such pretty *eyes!*'" Wroxy's laugh sounded like a short bark. "What they really mean is, 'Oh, too bad you're so fat because otherwise you're not completely fuck-ugly.'"

"I think you're beautiful." And then he'd added timidly, "*I'd* have sex with you."

Wroxy had smiled. She'd looked at him in the mirror and said, "No, you wouldn't, baby, but thanks for saying it anyway. I appreciate the compliment all the same."

"I *would!*"

"No, you wouldn't. And you know why, too, so stop it."

"Why?" Mikey had asked, dreading what her answer would be, also suspecting that Wroxy was too kind to make him feel small by using words in this particular context that would not be retractable later. Although they were the same age, Wroxy seemed more like a big sister. The fact that she genuinely seemed not to care what people thought of her, when Mikey cared passionately about what people thought of him and, in fact, was desperate to be liked or even loved, occasionally created a gulf between them. On one side was Wroxy cheerfully giving Auburn the finger; on the other was Mikey, gaping in reverential wonder at her courage, at the same time half-wishing he was part of the cliques she was giving the finger to.

"Just because," Wroxy said lightly. She smudged her purple lipstick with her little finger and checked the effect in the mirror with a practiced, critical eye. "Hand me my shawl, would you?"

"Tell me!"

"Mikey, do you really want to talk about this now?"

"I want to know what you meant," Mikey pleaded. "Please."

What had followed was the most intimate discussion Mikey had ever had with anyone. Wroxy told him that it had been obvious to her for some time that he wasn't interested in girls, and that it was okay with her. "Hell," she'd said, "it's even kind of cool." On the nights that she'd manage to sneak away from Auburn to Toronto and the Goth clubs on Queen Street, she'd seen a lot of gay guys and their boyfriends. It was no big deal in the real world, just here in this shitty little redneck town.

"How do you know I'm not interested in girls?" Mikey had asked. It was a weak *pro forma* effort at a last-ditch defence of his manhood. He was torn between the sense of a huge weight being lifted off his shoulders and a Pandora's box of secret desires being opened and released once and for all. He felt giddy and lightheaded at the same time, and his belly seemed gravid with dread. Knowing or suspecting something, especially about oneself, wasn't the same thing as saying it out loud.

"Look, baby," Wroxy said, sitting down on the bed and taking Mikey's hands in hers. "Sometimes girls know about gay guys even before gay guys know. You following me so far?"

Mikey nodded, wide-eyed. He wasn't remotely following her, but he was spellbound, nonetheless, by the possibilities her words implied, possibilities he hadn't dared to entertain. *I'm not gay. I'm not gay. I'm not gay.*

And then: *Am I?*

"It's like this. You're a sensitive guy, you don't play sports, and the jocks hate you." She laughed at that. Wroxy detested jocks. "You're more like a girl in a lot of ways, and maybe that's one of the reasons you and I are best friends. We like the same sort of stuff—the Anne Rice books, the music . . ." Wroxy paused. "Well, maybe not music. I can't stand that Madonna and Mariah Carey shit you love so much. But even still, we're a lot alike. Look at us here this afternoon, for instance. You're not out playing hockey or even hanging around the Milton Mall trying to pick up girls. You're watching me put on my makeup like it's the most amazing thing you've ever seen. If you ever wanted to try it, you know . . ." Her voice was tentative and gentle, as though she were afraid to offend him, or spook him, or break the spell. She let go of his hands and gestured toward the pots and tubes that littered her dressing table. "That would be, like, totally cool with me. I've seen makeup on Goth guys at the club, and it looks great."

Mikey stared at her. He felt as though he had fallen down an elevator shaft, or off a cliff, and was testing his body to see which bones he had broken. For some reason, he didn't feel as though any bones were broken. So far, all seemed to be intact. He began to cry.

"Oh my God," Wroxy said, horrified. "I'm so sorry, Mikey. Hey . . . hey . . . please don't cry. I feel like shit now. Oh my God, I knew I should have kept my big fucking mouth shut." She stood up clumsily and banged her knee on an open dresser drawer. She shouted, "*Fuck!*" Wroxy rummaged through her cosmetics case in search of a tissue. She found one that was clean, if crumpled, and handed it to Mikey who dabbed delicately at his eyes. "Okay, look. Just ignore everything I just said if you want, okay?"

"Well, what if I am . . . gay?" Mikey was sobbing. "What if it's . . . wrong? What if I go to hell?"

Wroxy laughed uproariously. She hugged him. Mikey smelled sandalwood perfume oil and cigarettes.

"What do you mean *go* to hell?" she said. "You're *in* hell already, Mikey." Wroxy laughed again, and this time the laugh sounded a little darker. "That's what this town is. It doesn't get any worse than this, and it gets a fuck of a lot better someday when we get the hell *out*. You watch. Jesus, listen to you—'go to hell.' You sound like one of the Holy Stripers." Wroxy giggled. She picked up her purse from the floor and reached into it. She pulled out a joint and looked up at the ceiling guiltily. Wroxy lit the joint, inhaling deeply. She blew out a plume of sickly sweet smoke.

"Are you nuts?" Mikey was shocked. "Your mother can smell that!"

"My mother has been smoking cancer sticks her entire life. She can barely smell her own shit in the morning."

Mikey giggled. Wroxy extended the joint to him, but he shook his head in prim refusal, thinking of what would happen at home if his mother smelled pot on his clothes. Donna Childress didn't smoke, and she could smell pot a mile away. She called it a gateway drug.

"My mom sure as hell isn't going to smell this little joint. Besides," Wroxy added, "I'll tell her it's a new perfume."

"Make sure you spray something around the room to kill the smell anyway," Mikey said, fretting. "It smells pretty strong and your mother isn't stupid. She'll know it isn't a new perfume."

"Whatever," Wroxy said. She sounded bored with the topic. She took another drag. "Dude, I think you just came out."

"*What*? What does that *mean*?"

"Mikey, chill." Wroxy sighed. "You're so uptight. I've never seen you this uptight. 'Coming out' is what they call it when gay guys and lesbians tell someone they're gay."

"I didn't tell *you* I was gay, you told *me* I was gay. It's not the same thing."

"So you're not gay?" Wroxy made a wry face. "Mikey, I'm your best friend. I won't tell anyone, but honestly, don't you think it's better this way? We can talk, like, honestly. You can tell me about what it's like when you like a guy and you're gay, and I can tell you what it's like when I like a guy and he's . . . well, I don't like any guys in Auburn. They're all losers."

"Not all of them," Mikey said softly, thinking of Jim Fields, who had broken his heart, but whom he still pined for and yearned to forgive.

"Name one," Wroxy challenged him. "Name one nice guy from among the assholes who beat you up and call you a faggot every day, or call me a whore and a Satan worshipper."

Mikey was silent. He realized that clandestine crushes on his male classmates, however pleasant they might be in his daydreams and night fantasies, weren't the same thing as being able to say that the boys he was in love with were nice people.

"I didn't think so," Wroxy said smugly.

"Don't you ever wish you had a boyfriend? I mean, don't you ever wish you were in love?"

"Please," she said. "I have the rest of my life to fall in love."

"I don't feel like I have the rest of my life to fall in love. I want to be in love now. I want what everyone else has."

Wroxy snorted. "Not another word about love until you admit some things, Mikey. Not another word from me until you say, 'Wroxy, I'm gay.' I'm fucking serious, dude. Either we're best friends or we aren't."

"Of course we're best friends," Mikey said weakly. "You know that. But . . ."

"No 'buts,' Mikey." Then, softening. "Please?"

Mikey took a deep breath and closed his eyes. "I'm gay," he said. He exhaled. The air came out as a shudder.

Wroxy stood up and crossed over to where he was sitting on the floor. She stroked his hair lightly with one hand, then gently lifted his chin up so he was looking in her eyes.

"Thank you," she said gently. She embraced him, pulling Mikey in close. He inhaled her comfortable scent.

"Please, please, please don't tell anyone," he pleaded. "I trust you.

I don't trust anyone else. People would kill me if they knew about this."

"Don't worry," Wroxy promised. "This is our secret. And it'll be so much better now, too. We'll be like sisters."

"I may be gay," Mikey said indignantly. "But that doesn't make me a girl. It doesn't make us *sisters*."

"Oh, Mikey," Wroxy said in her most world-weary tone. "You have so much to learn about the vernacular of gay people. You know what *vernacular* means, right?"

"Of course I do," said Mikey, who didn't, but wasn't about to let on. "So what?"

"Gay guys often call each other 'sisters,' and they call their girl-friends—their friends who are girls—'sisters.'"

"Where do you get this stuff? I mean, I've never even heard this shit, and I'm the one who's supposed to be gay."

"Oh, at the clubs in the city most of the girls have guy friends who are gay. You pick this stuff up, you know. It'll happen to you, too, once you get out of this shitty town and start hanging around with people who are genuinely cool, not fakes like these veal calves in Auburn. One of these nights you have to sneak away from your house so we can go to the city and hit Queen Street. I'm going to take you to a fetish night at one of the Goth clubs."

"One step at a time, Wroxy." Internally, he reeled between euphoria and dread. *I'm gay. I'm gay. I'm gay. I actually said it out loud.* "I just told you the biggest secret of my life. I've never told anyone else. I haven't even admitted it to myself in actual words."

Wroxy said, "Mikey, congratulations. And Happy Birthday."

"It's not my birthday. My birthday is in August."

"It's your birthday," Wroxy said, smiling. "You just came out. Trust me, it's your birthday. This is the first day of your real life."

"I would die for love. I would kill for it."

"I know you would." The voice is soft and low. Smooth, unrushed.

The large, warm hand caresses his cheek with a lover's knowing, insinuating playfulness. Strong fingers trace the underside of his jaw and chin, then trail off. He feels warm breath against his neck, then he hears a regretful sigh as the hand pulls away.

"Soon, Mikey."

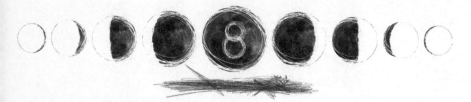

His eyes snapped open on darkness.

Mikey looked up at the ceiling of his bedroom. His temples throbbed, and it felt like there was a band of razor wire wound around his forehead. The staleness of the bedroom was stifling, the torpid heat pressing against his chest like a large, shaggy animal breathing damp foulness into his face. He looked at the digital clock on his night table. It was nine o'clock at night. Mikey realized that he had once again fallen asleep praying for love.

How fucking pathetic.

And here he was now, wide awake, sweaty, and with the beginnings of a blasting headache. Mikey looked toward his bedroom window. It was closed, which accounted for the ungodly heat. Switching on his night table lamp, he swung his legs over the side of the bed and stood up, crossing the floor to the window. He fumbled with the bolt, pushing it upward till he heard the click of the latch, then pushed the window wide open.

A cool breeze fanned his face. Mikey looked out and saw that the grass of the back lawn was tinted golden-yellow. The shadows of the yard had receded, and he could see the edges of the trees bordering the farthest part of the lawn, the picnic table, lawn chairs, all with preternatural clarity in the shimmering amber phosphorescence. Still groggy from sleep, he wondered what he was seeing.

Then he looked up.

A swollen yellow moon, full and low, hung heavily in the dark-violet sky. It burned above Auburn like a headlight, the sullen, dying-fire light that pulsed from its dark yellow heart tingeing, rather than illuminating, what it touched. An ocean of empurpled black clouds churned majestically about the moon's edges like a vast ash-coloured ocean.

Mikey stared at it in awe. "Holy shit," he whispered. He backed away from the window, bumping his calves on the bedframe. Mikey reached behind him and switched off the light beside his bed, plunging the room into its former blackness, except now the umber light from the moon stole through the glass and crept across the floor. When the telephone rang, he actually jumped.

"Hey, it's me, Wrox," came the familiar raspy voice. "Dude, have you looked outside? Look at the moon. It's awesome. If you haven't seen it yet, look out your window."

"I'm looking at it right now," Mikey breathed. "I've never seen anything like it. It's beautiful. It looks like it's about two feet away from the earth. It's a harvest moon."

"It's not a harvest moon," Wroxy said. "Nobody harvests in August. The harvest moon is in September, the hunter's moon is in October. The moon you're looking at right now is called a sturgeon moon."

"Whatever," Mikey said. "It's beautiful."

"Deborean witches call the August moon the fruit moon, but generally Wiccans call it the sturgeon moon because it's sturgeon season in many parts of the world. It's generally thought of as a moon cycle during which witches give thanks. They don't just give thanks to the Spirit, they give thanks to themselves and one another as well. It's a magical night, you know. You should meditate. I'm going to light some candles after a while and visualize. You want to come over?"

Mikey was still staring out the window, enthralled. He felt that if he reached out right now, he could touch the moon's waxy yellow face.

"Um, no thanks, Wrox. I'm going to go out for a little while. Maybe ride my bike, I've been cooped up all afternoon in the house. I fell asleep and woke up with a massive headache. I think some fresh air would be really good for me about now."

"You don't want to come over?" She sounded disappointed. "You want me to come with you?"

"No thanks, Wroxy. I really do think I need to be alone for a while. How about tomorrow?"

"Okay, suit yourself," she said petulantly. "Have a good night. Call me tomorrow if you want. We should hang out. School starts in a week and a half, and we're going to have to deal with those assholes soon enough. We should spend some time together before it happens."

"I'll call you, I promise. Night, honey."

Mikey hung up the phone before Wroxy could even say good-night. He was dimly aware of the fact that this had likely hurt her feelings, but he was less bothered by the possibility than he might have been at another time. His overriding need and sole driving purpose at that moment was to get out of the house and into the night, under that moon, away from the town and into the hills above Auburn where he could experience it in all of its glory.

Mikey stepped out into the hallway and glanced toward his parents' bedroom. The door was closed, and no light shone beneath it. The hallway was similarly dark and silent. Neither of them was home, clearly. He went down the stairs. The house was exceedingly dark and quiet, the heavy air unmoving. From the living room he heard the ticking of the grandfather clock in the corner by the fireplace,

It was Wednesday night, and he remembered his mother saying that she would be late coming home from church. As for his father, it was anyone's guess where Larry Childress would be at this hour. Lately, he had been spending less and less time at home with his family. Mikey had noticed a growing tension between his parents, owing largely to his mother's involvement with the Assembly, yet Mikey felt guilty about it. He supposed, as unpopular children often do, that it was somehow connected to him. He felt his parents' disappointment and opprobrium with every one of his mother's long, deep sighs, and with every wince from his father when Mikey burst out with something excitedly at the dinner table—usually something that had to do with a horror movie he wanted to see, or a new Anne Rice or Stephen King novel he had just read, or an actress he idolized.

"Boys don't squeal like that, son," Larry had told him once when Mikey had interrupted a conversation he and his mother had been having about an illness in the next-door neighbour's family. Mikey had been thirteen, and he'd thought his parents' conversation was over. His father had banged his fists on the table, and Mikey had flinched. "They speak calmly and steadily, and they think about what they're about to say. And they don't *giggle*."

"Dad, I think about what I want to say," Mikey had replied, chastened. "Sometimes it just comes out in a hurry."

"You need to learn some control, Mikey. You can't just go through life interrupting conversations at the dinner table with a lot of babble that you haven't thought out."

"Larry, please." His mother's voice had been pained. "Can we just have a nice dinner as a family for a change?"

Mikey had looked gratefully at his mother, but there was no warmth in her face, just tired irritation, and embarrassment at her son. It was also obvious that she blamed Mikey for provoking his father, not just his father for reprimanding him. Mikey looked down, shamefaced.

"Mikey, Brother Cowell and I were praying about you the other day," Donna began. "We were asking the Lord to help you with your loneliness and your isolation from the other boys. Brother Cowell thinks that maybe if you played more sports or joined the church's young men's club, you might be able to find yourself."

"Why were you talking about me with your pastor?" Mikey was confused. He had only seen Kelvin Cowell once or twice, and he doubted very much that the man even know who he was.

"He asked about you, Mikey," his mother said proudly. "He says he takes an interest in you. Maybe you should come to church with me next Wednesday. You might like it. There are very nice kids there."

"I don't think so, Mom, but thanks for asking."

"Well, you think about it, Mikey. Brother Cowell says it's never too late to turn to the Lord. With your problems," she added pointedly. "And your questions."

"I'm trying to teach the boy how to get on in the world, Donna," his father said, raising his voice. "He can't go on thinking it's okay to giggle like a girl or interrupt conversations with a lot of bullshit about Hollywood or crap horror books. Sometimes I think we have a daughter, not a son. Pray about *that* next time you're at that church of yours, but don't drag him into that freak show. The kid has enough strikes against him already." His father had made a disgusted sound, thrown his napkin on the table, stood up, and left the room. Donna had sighed and begun clearing the plates.

And then, like all other such encounters with his parents, Mikey had simply folded the memory of it into a cache of memories so similar that he wondered if some day he would cease to be able to tell them apart.

Mikey walked along the downstairs hallways, crossing the living room floor in the dark. He didn't bother to switch the light on. His mother believed that leaving lights on was a waste of electricity, which was also why they didn't have air-conditioning in the house, but not turning the lights on had nothing to do with obeying his mother. He simply preferred the darkness. In the dining room the moonlight surged through the windows like an orange tide. He walked through the dining room's swinging doors into the kitchen. He opened the kitchen door that led to the backyard and stepped outside.

Mikey imagined he could feel the moon's weight as he opened the garage door and pulled out his bicycle. He wanted the wind against his face. He climbed on and began to pedal as fast as he could away from the house, into the arms of the night.

There are monsters in small towns, but you have to look hard to find them, especially after dark. They hide with the sort of cunning that would be unnecessary in a large city where it is infinitely easier to blend in, where the sheer number of people who live side by side forms a sort of barrier, a camouflage of humanity among which the inhumane can burrow during daylight hours, rising at night to pursue their carious, savage hungers on dark, unlit streets and alleyways. In small towns, though, red mischief tends to hide behind closed doors—the horrors of incest, of wife battery, of emotional cannibalism and neglect, or the crushing of dreams by parents who thought they were doing the right thing when stamping the light out of their children with raised, shaming voices and stinging slaps.

Mikey had no sense of this as he pedalled his bike through the shadow-dappled streets of Auburn that smelled of late-summer roses, past the sensible, prim brick houses with the neatly tended lawns whose very probity was an insistent declaration of virtue. He pedalled past those houses, slowing down and pausing when he saw shadows moving against the soft lamplight behind drawn curtains, or when he heard the susurrus of muffled voices, or occasional drunken laugh, coming from behind a patio fence where respectable people might be enjoying a barbecue.

He pedalled on through the night, the yellow moon overhead like the all-seeing eye of God.

Mikey would have no way of knowing, for instance, that buried in the fields that lay half a mile directly behind Stash and Yalda Verbinski's impeccably maintained split-level on Dagenais Street lay the bodies of three cats, a raccoon, and a dog that Dewey had killed over the past three years, or that this act of ultimate power over smaller and weaker creatures gave him a thrill unequal to any he had ever known. Or that inside the very presentable house, as Dewey went through the day-to-day motions of trying to be a dutiful son to his parents and somehow earn his father's love and approval, a separate reality existed behind his eyes, running like a movie full of slaughter, a movie in which Dewey was the hero of a world on fire, with rivers of blood running at his feet. Or that sometimes he wondered if Johnny Treleaven would make the same helpless squealing sound the raccoon made when Dewey had plunged the knife into its belly and watched its insides tumble out like soggy red rope, or if a person sounded different when they died.

Mikey swept past the Verbinski house, pedalling a little faster, sensing danger as he always did when he was in close proximity to Dewey.

He turned left from Dagenais onto Welland Avenue, then pedalled out toward Main Street.

He similarly would have no way of knowing, for instance, that the Reverend Kelvin Cowell, whose rigorously plain house he had just passed on Welland, kept a stack of violent bondage pornography in a locked trunk in his basement. Or that although he had made his prison-to-Jesus conversion story the engine that drove his ministry, the fact that he'd been in jail for burglary, not murder, was an irony that never ceased to tickle him when he thought of the two female hitchhikers he had raped and stabbed to death in the back of his Ford truck in Saskatchewan and British Columbia in 1953 and 1957, respectively. He'd buried the first girl, a bouncy, fat redhead named Brenda, in a swampy muskeg beneath a copse of coniferous trees that he could still picture in his mind when he masturbated, thinking of her decayed face and the moss that now likely covered her unmarked grave and maybe even her skeleton; the second, a sad, jaundiced, wormy-looking girl named Melanie, who had given him similar thrills, lay beneath six feet of stony earth in the heart of a dark forest in the mountains outside of Invermere. Knowing that he would die with the sole knowledge of where the bodies had been buried made him feel like a god, and he had an artist's pride in the fact that he had never been caught.

When he'd been arrested and incarcerated for his break-and-enter in Ontario in 1963, it had naturally not occurred to the police to connect him to the two unsolved murders on the other side of the country. Why would they? Kelvin Cowell had no previous record, nor had he ever been accused of, or charged with, any violent act. He'd served his sentence at the penitentiary in Kingston, patiently planning how he would "find Jesus" toward the middle of his incarceration, then spin it into a career once he was out. After all, a man needed a job and a purpose, and Cowell knew he wasn't getting any younger. If any of his congregants caught him glancing wolfishly at their whey-faced daughters, their budding breasts concealed beneath smock-like modesty dresses, they would ascribe it to a man's natural hunger, also a gift from God. They privately (and not so privately) wondered when the Lord would send their handsome, God-fearing pastor a helpmeet to aid him in his wondrous work. For even as Adam cleaved to Eve, they said a man must leave his mother and cleave to a wife.

If any of the Holy Stripers had seen the true shape of Cowell's desires, or the pointy communion he dreamed of late at night when he touched himself, thinking of the two dead women who had given him so much pleasure, they might have doubted God's love itself.

But Mikey wouldn't know any of that as he pedalled past, and out onto the open dirt road that led out of Auburn. When he passed the abandoned graveyard at the very outer edge of town, he turned his bike toward the cliffs of the escarpment that framed the grinning yellow moon like great fingers of rock.

Mikey smelled the bonfire before he saw the shower of sparks exploding in the air above the meadow as he crested the brow of the hill. He squeezed the brakes. The bike stopped so abruptly that it almost threw him. He regained his balance, putting both feet on the road, then crouched on the side of the road overlooking the meadow. Though Mikey didn't immediately realize what he was looking at, his heart still caught in his chest with some primordial knowledge. Then, when he saw the figures in black robes undulating slowly around the fire—Mikey counted eleven—he knew it consciously as well.

He was looking at the witches of Auburn, in the flesh.

Much later he would wonder how he had known so surely how to navigate the moonlit roads in that weird yellow twilight, but in that instant he knew only that he was actually *seeing* something that he'd only ever heard about in gossip, or dreamed about when the day-to-day reality of his life had grown too unbearable.

And he was suddenly very, very cold.

Mikey wrapped his arms around his torso, wishing he had worn a sweater or a jacket, only barely remembering that the night had been suffocatingly hot in his room an hour earlier, and that there had only been a slight breeze when he'd stepped outside his house to get his bicycle from the garage. His t-shirt had been dampish and had dried slightly in the night air as he'd pedalled. Now it clung to his torso and back, chilling him. The temperature seemed to have dropped several degrees in the spot where he was standing, and he began to shiver. Acting on instinct, Mikey moved his body around the boulder toward the distant fire burning about fifty yards away from where he crouched. The instant he moved from his spot, the air warmed perceptibly. Then the spectral cold reached for him again, pulling him back into its chill grasp like a possessive suitor.

When he felt gelid fingers caress the skin of his neck and trace a line down the centre of his back, he barely stifled a scream.

Mikey whirled around, turning his head from side to side, but there was no one standing behind him. For a moment he thought he heard mocking male laughter carried on the breeze, but whatever the sound had actually been, it tattered away into the dark, and all he could hear was the wind high in the trees at his back and, now, the rising murmur of chanting voices coming from the black-robed figures in the meadow swaying rhythmically, hands joined, faces raised to the moon, and the shower of sparks that burst from the bonfire, shattering against the black night sky.

As his eyes became accustomed to the division between firelight, moonlight, and darkness, he saw a cluster of vans and cars at the outer perimeter of the bonfire.

The crowd parted as a twelfth figure, taller than the others and wearing a crimson robe and some sort of crown decorated with what looked like antlers or horns, walked toward the group at a stately, measured pace from beyond the edge of the firelight.

Mikey watched as the figure—he guessed it was a man, based on its height and the breadth of its shoulders—dragged something along on the end of a rope behind him. For one horrible moment, Mikey thought it might be a white dog, but then he saw that it was a goat. The animal seemed confused and frightened by the fire. It bleated occasionally but otherwise seemed trusting, as though it were the man's pet. He led the goat into the centre of the crowd, next to the fire, as the others formed a semicircle.

The man pushed the animal roughly into the dirt. Two of the black-robed figures stepped forward and knelt, holding the animal down. One held the goat's neck, the other held its back legs and hooves. The goat began to bleat frantically, but the chanting that rose in crescendo drowned out its cries.

From inside his crimson robe, the man with the crown of horns withdrew a knife. Its blade flashed in the firelight as he brought it down in a slashing arc across the goat's throat, severing the carotid artery, releasing a shower of blood. The animal stopped struggling. It shuddered once, then was still.

Mikey felt his bladder empty itself warmly into his jeans at the exact moment he stumbled backward, turned, and vomited. The stench of his bile blossomed against the earth like a rich, sickening flower. His stomach heaved again and again till it was empty and his legs were soaked with his own warm piss.

He wiped a dribble of puke off his mouth with his hand and looked back.

A woman had stepped forward out of the circle. She carried a bowl in her hands. They looked very white against the draped black sleeves of her robe. Delicately, as though she was dipping a cup into a punch bowl at a tea party, the woman leaned forward and caught some of the blood still gushing from the animal's severed neck. The blood looked black in the firelight. The woman bowed to the man with the knife, who was now standing over the goat's lifeless body, and handed the bowl to him. Then she walked back to the circle and joined hands with the others.

The witches—for by now, Mikey, in the throes of the whitest terror and no longer in any position to think of them any other way—formed a complete circle around the horned man and waited in apparent anticipation. The man raised the bowl to his lips and drank from it. When he raised his head, there were dark smears around his mouth, and his cheeks were stained. Then he raised his arms. He appeared to be offering the bowl to something overhead. Mikey looked up, but saw nothing. Reverently, the witches waited, looking up into the night sky.

Mikey first felt the hairs rise on his arms, then he felt as though he'd lost the ability to see or hear, felt sucked into a soundless vacuum.

In the distance he saw the glow of the lights of town. Raising his head farther, he saw that the moon was slightly down, but otherwise the sky was clear. Higher up, he saw the stars, bright in the country dark in a way that they never were in the city.

The air had grown thick and heavy and silent, the way it did before thunderstorms in the summer, pregnant and huge with coiled power about to spring. Mikey smelled ozone and something like the odour of just-lit matches, or old pennies, sulfurous and metallic and sour.

Lightning flickered at the centre of a boiling, tenebrous bank of clouds in the air directly above the witches. The clouds thickened and darkened and began to spin in a lazy, hypnotic vortex. Mikey knew that what he was seeing was impossible. Storm clouds didn't form *beneath* a clear night sky, and lightning didn't flash five hundred feet in the air.

He heard a gasp from the assembly, but it trailed off into a sort of sigh of something like ecstasy, and they began to sway in unison as though they could hear music that he could not.

Faster and faster the clouds swirled and danced, shaping themselves into forms that looked vaguely human, then grotesquely inhuman. The lightning flickered inside the pulsing heart of the cloud bank like a mischievous child playing with a powerful flashlight inside a tent. The smell of sulfur grew stronger and Mikey felt himself gagging again. He covered his mouth with his hand, willing his stomach to calm itself.

Mikey knew that if any of the black-robed figures around the fire discovered him hiding behind the boulder, they would kill him. It was late at night, and he was miles from home. He would vanish, and no one would ever hear from him again.

Then he felt the ground under his feet begin to tremble. The lightning inside the clouds turned red and exploded across the meadow, bathing the trees, the ground and the rocks in aureate light. From the centre of the boiling mist, a massive column in the rough shape of a man's arm formed itself from the shifting bank of necromantic fog. The arm grew distinctly human in form, powerfully muscled and fully formed with an encompassing hand that ended in long, taloned fingers.

The hand flexed once, then plucked the bowl held aloft, pulling it up into the cloud bank. The hand reached down again and pulled the butchered body of the goat by its hind legs into the air. Mikey clearly saw the gaping wound at the animal's severed throat as the head lolled at a grotesque angle, the fur clotted with gore, matted nearly black in the area closest to the wound. He saw the goat's forelegs hanging suspended for a second. Then its body disappeared into the cloud bank.

And then, something like an enormous face formed of cloud and shadow, with eyes like red lightning, leaned down and smiled in benediction with a mouth full of terrible teeth. Then it, too, vanished into the fog.

The effect on the witches was immediate and devastating. They dropped reverently to their knees and raised their supplicant arms toward the thing in the cloud above their heads, chanting and shouting in a language Mikey had never heard before.

As he watched, they removed their robes, revealing nude bodies of every shape and age. Casting the garments aside, they began to half-shuffle, half-skip around the fire. They linked arms and hands as they reached up, then bent low in an orgasmic spiral dance. Breaking away, one of the younger men grabbed a woman with long grey hair and sagging breasts and threw her slack, puckered body to the ground, into the puddle of gore where the goat had been slaughtered. Mikey watched his muscular back and rear flex and buck as he fucked the old woman hard, her legs circling his solid, tattooed midsection, pulling him in closer. When he flipped her over and mounted her from the rear, Mikey saw that her back was slick with the animal's blood. Two men faced each other and began to grind their naked bodies against each other. Entwined in each other's arms, they sank to the ground and they, too, began to fuck. Others joined in, and soon the ground was a mass of writhing, entwined limbs.

Above them the cloud began to dissipate, breaking off into shreds of vapour, and the flickering lightning grew weaker, flashing dully now like dirty brass. Then it, too, dissipated.

Mikey forced himself to tear his gaze from the orgy and look up. He became aware that, as the swirling fog blew away, he could again hear the natural sounds of the night. The pressure of the air had likewise lifted. He looked around at the dark forest behind him, beyond the border of rocks on the side of the road above the meadow.

He smelled August—humidity and the promise of rain. The scent of sulfur lingered briefly in the air, and then it was simply . . . *not* there. The air above the tangled mass of bodies was now completely clear, lit only by moonlight and the reflected glow from the bonfire.

Backing away slowly, crouched low, keeping close to the shadows and praying the darkness would cover his path, Mikey reached for his bicycle and brought it upright. The grinding of the rubber tire against the dirt and twigs as he walked his bike backward, away from the meadow, sounded deafening.

Mikey.

He stopped in his tracks and stood completely still. The whisper had seemed to come from all around him, and yet at the same time it was as though it ricocheted in his mind through some sort of mental echo chamber.

His brain registered dread, then circumvented that dread in order to facilitate survival as his body went into the full fight-or-flight mode he'd studied in biology class. His pupils were dilated and his veins sang with adrenaline as blood was shunted away from the digestive tract and directly into his limbs. His sight sharpened, and his impulses felt quickened, muscles coiled. He knew that if he jumped on his bicycle right now, it would feel like flying.

Mikeeeeeeey.

The brain-sound of his name shivered through his mind like the dry rattle of dark leaves tossed by the wind. The witches were staring at him, and he knew beyond any shadow of a doubt that they could see him. Some were squatting on their haunches, others had paused in their rutting and propped themselves up on their elbows and knees, heads turned in his direction. Others rose to a standing position and stood with their arms hanging at their sides.

There was a hum in the air that made him think about the time, as an eight-year old, some bigger kids had tricked him into entering a fenced-in compound surrounding a power station near his house. That day, as he'd stared at the *DANGER* sign and the line drawing of a male figure prone on the ground with crude lightning bolts firing toward his body, he'd been aware of the massive surge of raw energy that thrummed through the ground.

It was like that now. He felt twelve pairs of terribly knowing eyes on his body. Intellectually he knew it was impossible. He was too deeply in the shadows of the tree line near the road. And yet they saw him. He knew they did. He could *feel* it.

Then the man in the crimson robe took a step forward, away from the others, toward Mikey. He raised his arm and waved with a colloquial familiarity that would not have been out of place in a mall parking lot or a movie theatre. In his hand the twelve-inch blade still clotted with blood and fur glittered redly in the firelight. Although the hood covered the upper part of his face, the lower half was completely visible.

The man was grinning.

Mikey swung his legs over the sides of his bike and launched himself in the direction of the road with a force that almost pitched him over his handlebars.

He didn't look back. He didn't want to see what might be there if he did.

Mikey had never pedalled faster in his life, nor had he ever felt more like he was flying, nor had flight ever been less of a luxury or a fantasy. When the country roads had given way to the outskirts of town, he had not slowed down. It was only when he passed his first Tim Horton's doughnut shop, brightly lit inside and full of late-night truckers, shift-workers, and a couple of cops, that he had allowed himself to slow his pace slightly and coast. He careened through the residential streets till he got to his house on Webster Avenue, turning sharply into his driveway, recklessly swinging his legs off the bike and flinging it up against the wall of the garage. His father would have a cow in the morning and ask why the bike had been left out all night. He would think of something. The garage was dark, and Mikey didn't want to be in a dark place right now.

Inside the kitchen, the potpourri of familiar odours enveloped him like a blanket. His mother had cleaned the kitchen before she'd gone to bed, and the faint scent of Windex and dishwasher soap hung in the air. In the past, the smell might have never registered anything other than familiarity, but tonight it evoked everything sane and normal in a world suddenly poisoned by the night.

Now, in his room, Mikey sat up in his bed, back pressed against the wall, staring at the open bedroom door and the night-light from the hallway, a Bible clutched tightly to his chest as though it were a hot water bottle. He'd always kept the Bible on the bottom of his bookcase, wedged between a copy of Anton Szandor Lavey's *The Satanic Bible* and Gerald B. Gardner's 1954 classic, *Witchcraft Today*. Before tonight, Mikey had enjoyed the perverse irony of his Bible's placement. Now, though, as he waited for dawn, the irony wasn't even something he considered. He felt that if he let go of the Bible, he would be completely defenceless.

His terror was all encompassing, and his heart felt like it was straining to leave his chest. His bedroom had always felt safe to him. It had always been a haven. Tonight, though, he watched his bedroom window in dread. He'd left his door open not out of bravery but because he wanted to be able to hear the sound of scratching at the living room window or the rattle of anyone trying the doors in the house. He had double-checked the locks before mounting the stairs to his room, afraid to look out the windows as he passed them, but even more afraid not to.

The clock on his bedside table read four a.m. The house was silent except for the faint sound of his father snoring behind the closed bedroom door down the hall. When Mikey had been a little boy, he was comforted, as he drifted off to sleep, by the notion that there were adults awake in the house, adults who could protect him from anything in the nameless bestiary of childhood terrors.

But he doubted very much that the witches, or the monstrous thing in the cloud, would care too much about his father's might, or even his mother's religion.

Mostly though—and this was the worst part to Mikey—he knew that his father wouldn't believe a word of what had happened tonight. He didn't care, for once, about being believed for the sake of his vanity, or being taken seriously by his father. No, tonight it was about survival. And the fact that Mikey knew he had seen what he had seen, with no room for any doubt whatsoever, meant that he was completely alone against whatever walked in the forest at night.

He rolled his head on the pillow and stared at the telephone.

He wanted to call Wroxy. She was the only one who would understand what had happened and the only one who would believe him. Pragmatically he knew that if he called her house at four in the morning, he would wake her mother and then he would have to answer more questions than he was prepared to.

Mikey continued to stare at the telephone. He wondered if any of them had seen who he was. He wondered if under the black hoods and robes there were people he knew, people who had always known him. People who had been able to keep a side of their lives completely hidden from view. He wondered if the telephone would suddenly begin to ring in the dark house as his parents slept, as he lay in his bed, shivering, waiting for the dear, dear dawn.

And if the answering machine would click on downstairs in the kitchen, and if a low, savage, goat-killing voice would cut through the silent darkness of the house on Webster Avenue and say, *"Hello, Mikey Childress. Did you have fun tonight? We know you saw us. We saw you, too. We know who you are. And we're coming for you really, really soon."*

For the first time all summer, Mikey wept.

"You're telling me the truth, right?" Wroxy said, slack-jawed. "You're not lying, are you? Because if you are, I'm going to kill you. This is way too cool."

No, he assured her through a fresh torrent of tears, it was the truth.

They were sitting in Wroxy's basement bedroom. She'd been about to light candles, as she always did when they talked, when Mikey begged her not to.

"Please," he begged, crying. "I couldn't take it. I need to feel normal right now. Nothing weird. I couldn't take it.

Wroxy had sat in rapt attendance and listened while Mikey told her the most incredible story she had ever heard. Her initial response was to believe her friend, though maybe not about the arm and the face in the clouds, or the insinuating voices that had forced their way into his mind before he took off like a bat out of hell.

But as to the presence of the witches themselves, of that she had no doubt whatsoever. First off, Mikey was clearly terrified, so he had seen *something*. It all fit with everything she'd read on the Internet about the so-called witches of Auburn—the location, the twelve "witches," even the animal sacrifice. The information she'd already gleaned indicated that, if it even existed, this was no run-of-the-mill neo-pagan coven, but something darker and older, rooted in counter-Christianity and devil worship. While real pagans (and Wroxy considered herself a real pagan) looked askance at "Satan worship" as being the primary province of warped Christians, she could not deny the fact that the worship of the demonic existed, if not exactly flourished. And if, as she herself believed, there was no "black" or "white" magic, only what was in the heart of the witch, the heart of this group, based on what Mikey had told her as he wept anew, was dark indeed. Whatever else was true in Mikey's tale, the full moon last night would have been a source of immense power for anyone with the skill to use it properly. All of its power would then be drawn from that dark place. She thought of the slaughtered goat.

"Okay, have you thought of going to the police with this story?" Wroxy asked him when he calmed down. "First off, whatever else they were, they weren't actually witches."

"What were they then? Shriners? The Legion? And what about the thing I saw in that cloud? Have you been listening to me, Wroxy? *They killed a goat in front of me and drank its blood!*"

"Mikey," Wroxy began patiently. "I know you *think* you saw what you saw . . ."

"I *did* see what I saw, goddamnit!" he shouted. "And I'm fucking scared that they saw me and that they know who I am. They're *witches*, for Christ's sake. Who *knows* what they can do? Oh God, I'm so *fucked!*"

"Listen. First off, they weren't witches, okay? They were, like, perverts or something. You got scared by a bunch of freaks in black robes. I'd be freaked out, too, if I saw something like that. Real witches don't kill animals, and they don't do bad shit. It's bad karma if they do. Real witches are like me—they're peaceful and politically aware, and they light candles and cast spells for good. Are you following me so far?" Mikey nodded, and she continued. "On the other hand, even if they weren't actual *witches* with actual *powers*, they were the sort of people who have no trouble killing an animal for fun and drinking its blood. Have you thought about going to the police with this?" she asked again. "I mean, it's probably, like, a crime or something to kill an animal, right? How about cruelty to animals?"

"Listen, Wroxy, I know what I saw. I can't help it if you don't believe me, but I thought if anyone would believe me, you would."

"I do," she said earnestly. "But I think that some other stuff got mixed up in what you saw and what you didn't see. It was a weird night with that big moon, and it was late, and you were tired, and you were scared out of your wits. If I'd been there, I would have seen things, too."

"What about the cloud in the air?" Mikey's voice was plaintive, wanting to be reassured. "What about the face?"

"Smoke from the fire? How about that?"

Mikey paused to consider that possibility. It made rational sense.

"You said it was a big fire, right?" Wroxy added, encouraged by his silence as he pondered. At this point she was most disturbed by the dread she had seen in Mikey's face. She had seen Mikey upset before, especially after any bruising encounter with Dewey Verbinski, or some other casual cruelty by one of his schoolmates, but she had never seen him as pale as he was right now. Wroxy liked to play the tough downtown chick trapped in the sticks, but underneath the black clothing and the Goth makeup there was immense tenderness. "They probably put some green branches in there by mistake and made a lot of smoke. That would look weird at night, especially when you were already freaked out by what you were seeing. And," she added, warming to the soothing effect it was having on Mikey, "maybe there were some chemicals in the fire. You know, like something to make the flames go in different colours."

"The flames were normal," Mikey said, calming down. "It was everything else that wasn't normal."

"Babe, you had a bad scare. But look outside." She pointed to the window of her basement room from which ground-level sunlight leaked like weak tea through the smudged glass. "It's daylight now. There's nothing bad out there."

Mikey shivered. "I don't know that for sure. Wroxy?"

"Yes, *Michael*?" She suppressed a smile. He hated the name, and no one ever called him that, except his parents when they were angry. "What is it, dear?"

"Do you think they'll come after me?" His voice was very small. He sounded like a little boy. It broke Wroxy's heart to hear him sound like that. "Do you think I should tell my parents?"

"That's two questions, dude," she said definitively. "And there are two answers, one apiece. No, I don't think they'll come after you. I don't think they saw you. It sounded like they were so into having sex with one another that they probably missed you completely. If you weren't a virgin, you'd understand what that's like and why they wouldn't just stop to peek at you. Besides, you were out of the light, you said. They couldn't have seen you."

She took a deep breath, knowing that the next set of truths was going to be more painful for him to hear because they would last long past the time when the confusion over his witch-hunting escapades faded away. "As for telling your parents, let's lay this out. Larry and Donna, who don't have the most imagination anyway, already think they're raising an axe murderer because of all the weird books you read and the horror stuff you—I mean *we*—are into. If you tell them that you were out on the night of the full moon riding your bike around Auburn looking for witches, much less that you found them killing animals out past Glen Eden, and then—oh wait!—some demon or something reached out of a cloud and pulled a goat's dead body into the air and—what? *Ate it*? Come on, Mikey," she said, more sharply than she intended. "What do *you* think? Do you think you should tell your parents, or do you think it's one of those moments you should keep between us? *You* tell *me*."

"You're right," he said thickly. "They'd never believe me. They'd just be angry."

Wroxy was silent. She reached for his hand and held it. His skin was warmer than it had been when he had pedalled over to her house an hour before.

As hurt as Mikey was by the realization that his parents' comfort and support in this instance, as in so many others, wasn't something he could count on, it did feel reassuringly normal. A world away from witches and slaughter and demons.

"Hey," Wroxy said slyly. "I have an idea."

"What?" Mikey eyed her suspiciously. Something in her tone suggested that the idea she was about to propose would appeal to her far more than to him.

"Look, you know what they say about trauma," she began. "It might help you if we went to the spot where you say you saw the witches, or whatever the hell those freaks were. We could, you know, look around. You could check out the spot, and you could see there's no way that any of them could have seen you." She paused. "What do you think?"

"I think you're whacked," he said. "I think you're asking me to go back and relive one of the most horrible nights of my life so that you can add something unforgettable to your Box of Shadows or whatever the hell you call that witch diary of yours."

"It's called a Book of Shadows," she said serenely. "And no, I was offering out of the goodness of my heart. Look, we'd be together. We could take our bikes out to the escarpment, and we could look for the place. I'd be there for you. Also, I could probably cast a protection spell so that if there was any lingering bad energy from their circle, it would be neutralized."

"Wroxy, they killed an animal there. I'm more worried about the idea that they'd still be there, or nearby. I'm worried that they might get a second chance to get a good look at me so they'd have a better idea of where to find me if they decided to do . . . something."

"Feed you to the cloud demon, you mean?" she said, poker-faced. "Or—wait for it!—pull you into the sex circle so you lose your virginity under the next full moon. Like some sort of virgin sacrifice, except instead of sacrificing the virgin, they sacrifice his virginity. You did say that there were a couple of gay guys doing it, didn't you? Did you, you know, see anything?"

She began to giggle. In spite of himself, Mikey felt the corners of his mouth twitching involuntarily as he tried not to join her laughter.

Wroxy is like that, Mikey thought. *It's impossible to not laugh when she laughs.* In that moment he realized that in his way, unconventional though it seemed to him at that moment in time, he loved her.

"Very funny, Wrox," he said, trying to keep a straight face, but failing. "I'm serious. I don't want to go back. And I don't want you to go, either."

"All right, I promise," she said. "But sometime, when you're feeling more like it, I want to talk about what you saw. I want to talk about who those people were, and what they were doing. You realize that you've seen something that people in this town talk about all the time, but you actually saw it. They're real. It's not just a story."

Suddenly Mikey wanted coffee very badly. "Wroxy, let's go to the Milton Mall and see if they're still serving breakfast at the Golden Griddle, okay? I'm hungry." He smiled wanly. Wroxy saw that he was still very pale, and there were dark brown circles under his eyes. "I didn't sleep very much last night," he said, reading her gaze.

"Let me get some money from my mom," Wroxy said. She was determined to get control of this runaway train and bring things back to normal. She peered into her mirror. "I think it's a little early for full-on whore makeup, don't you? Oh, fuck it," she said, reaching for her makeup bag. "Those hicks already think I'm a slut, I might as well dazzle them with it."

"Wrox?"

"Mikey?"

"I imagined most of it, didn't I?"

He thought of the goat, its throat slashed and gaping, being pulled up into the fog by that arm attached to nothing he could see, nothing his mind could conceive an alternate scenario to. Mikey looked at her for a moment, the horror of what he'd seen skipping across the black surface of his memory like an obsidian stone into his subconscious. He felt cold again, suddenly, although it was August and the basement wasn't as cool as it could have been. He wanted to be in the sunlight.

"Yeah, you did, Mikey," Wroxy said as she adjusted her lipstick in the mirror with her little finger. "And the rest of it can't hurt you. Remember that."

Later, in Milton, as he walked along Main Street, turning right onto Ontario Street and the Milton Mall, he realized that he was instinctively looking into the faces of every man and woman he passed with an intensity that was previously unknown to him. The sunlight was very bright, and his sleepless eyes burned, making him squint. Even if the witches hadn't seen him, as Wroxy assured him they hadn't, *he* had seen *them*. But he hadn't, really. They were hooded. In short, they could be anyone. One more layer of invisibility had been ripped away from Mikey like an outer layer of protective, living skin.

Wroxy stood in the early evening sunlight, still bright, but cooler in the shadow of the escarpment cliffs. The light had turned copper as summer reluctantly conceded its supremacy to the oncoming autumn. There was a chill in the air even in town, but up here, nearly ten miles outside of Auburn, the cold had sharper teeth. She heard the wind high up in the trees behind her, but other than that she was conscious of the vast, imperial silence of the meadow beside which she stood. Wroxy crossed her arms inside her warm fleece sweatshirt and shivered a little. She leaned her bike against the boulder that Mikey had described with his usual exquisite—*very gay*, she thought, smiling—detail.

She walked off the road and stepped down onto the path that led into the clearing. Directly ahead of her lay a circle of charred firewood and ash about twenty-four feet in circumference. Forty feet from the outer edge of the circle of ash there were tire tracks in the soft dirt of the meadow that led up to the embankment and vanished when they met the dirt road. Wroxy walked closer to the charred circle, because she had always been a curious girl and not afraid of very much. Suddenly her right foot slipped. She inhaled sharply. The ground all around her was dry—it had been for most of this long, rainless summer. There was no mud anywhere.

She looked down. Wroxy was standing in a patch of wet, dark earth. It was indeed mud, but it looked a richer brown than the soil around it. The dirt was reddish in colour, like molasses or wet rust. She gasped and drew her foot back as though she had stepped on a live wire.

The sun was sinking behind the cliffs. The shadows were growing longer, and it was already darker now than when she first reached the spot she'd promised Mikey she would never visit, directions to which she'd been able to wheedle out of him in his sleep-deprived state as she'd fed him coffee over breakfast at the mall. Wroxy reached inside her sweatshirt and withdrew her pentacle. She held it in front of her and closed her eyes, imagining an outward-spiral-ling ring of white light that surrounded her and the immediate area around her.

"Mother Goddess, come to me," she whispered, squeezing her eyes tightly. "I charge that this circle of light shield me from all forces that come to do me ill. I entreat that this be done correctly and for the good of all. So mote it be."

She squinted into the last vestiges of the setting sun in the west and turned her back on it, facing east, toward the tree line of the shadow-dappled forest. She reached into her pocket and felt around for the crystal jasper she always carried with her. Her crystal was an all-purpose amulet, one of several she kept in her room at home and never left the house without. She'd ordered the North American jasper stone from a gem wholesaler she'd found online. Jasper, according to Wroxy's books on witchcraft, protected the bearer against entities from any realm. She closed her fingers around its reassuring, cool smoothness, finding comfort in its familiarity as the wind stirred the tops of the darkening branches.

She closed her eyes and spoke softly but clearly.

"Beings of the Earth, Guardians of the North, I ask that you stand firm and protect me in this space." She paused, then spoke again. "Beings of Air, Guardians of the East, I ask that you stand firm and protect me in this space." She turned to the left. "Beings of Fire,

Guardians of the South, I ask that you stand firm and protect me in this space."

Wroxy turned fully around, eyes still closed, and faced in the direction where she knew the sun was finishing its descent behind the horizon. "Beings of Water, Guardians of the West, I ask that you stand firm and protect me in this space."

When she opened her eyes, it was near dark and she was alone. All around her, the night was coming alive. The dark mud at her feet looked black in the fading sunlight. Wroxy remembered what she'd told Mikey about counterbalance in the universe. She wondered what would happen if the balance shifted.

This is a bad place, Wroxy thought. She looked away from the circle of ash and reminded herself that she didn't believe in devils or demons. She walked to the centre of the circle she had drawn in her mind and spoke again. This time her voice was little more than a whisper.

"Ancient One," she intoned softly. "The One that binds all the elements into one, I ask that you stand firm and protect me in this space."

A small bit of white caught Wroxy's eye, and she leaned down to pick it up. It was a thin, ragged strip of raw flesh from which protruded a tuft of coarse white hair. At the root it was clotted with dried blood. A few feasting ants dropped from the piece of meat, while others angrily scurried up Wroxy's fingers. With a cry she dropped the disgusting thing, frantically rubbing her hand against her jeans. Wildly she looked up into the empty, dark blue air above the scorched hearth as a line from one of her favourite stories, Nathaniel Hawthorne's tale of dark witchcraft, "Young Goodman Brown," came to her, unbidden: *Unfathomable to mere mortals is the lore of fiends.*

The last of the dying sunlight glanced off the tops of the cliffs, then vanished from sight. Wroxy inclined her head toward the boulder where her bike was. Had it been that far away? She turned and walked briskly up the path that led to the road. Something—a shadow? A flurry of motion?—caught her attention just outside her peripheral line of sight. She spun around, staring into the gloom, but whatever she had seen was no longer there. She hurried up toward her bike. Wroxy was sure of one thing, at least. She would never tell Mikey that she'd been to this place, never mind what she suspected about it. Never, ever. It would be the death of him. Better that he try to forget what he'd seen. Better still that he never found out what she'd seen.

She reached inside her pocket to locate the stones among the jumble of keys and coins. She pulled a handful of debris out of her pocket. The jasper gleamed dully in what remained of the light. Wroxy closed her eyes and sighed with relief as she held it.

The stone jumped in her hand. The tingling warmed the tender flesh of her palm and radiated up her arm; at the same time, she felt the vibration in every part of her body.

Wroxy's eyes flew open. She drew a sharp breath, dropping the jasper on the ground as though it had burned her. A trail of eldritch green fire sparkled after the stone as it fell. For a few seconds, the jasper glowed on the ground like a trapped firefly. Then the unearthly light faded and died against the black earth of the forest floor.

In that moment, she believed what Mikey had told her—she believed everything.

Behind her in the night an owl barked and Wroxy screamed to wake the dead.

Right away, Dewey Verbinski and Jim Fields noticed that the faggot and his Satanist girlfriend were back in their sight lines. Mikey's survival instincts kicked in, and he rapidly computed that Dewey had put on nearly fifteen pounds of new muscle over the summer. Jim Fields (for whom Mikey still harboured a dreamy obsession that Wroxy, likely correctly and with stunningly precocious insight, dubbed "classically masochistic") seemed to have put on ten pounds of the same. On Dewey, with his thick neck and cold blue eyes, the new bulk just looked terrifying and ogreish. To Mikey's eye however, Jim looked more impossibly Apollonian than ever before as he strutted through the hallways of Auburn High in wonderfully faded Levis, books casually balanced on one lean hip.

I would die for love. Yes, I would die for it.

"Look at those *arms*," Mikey whispered under his breath to Wroxy as they passed Jim in the hallway and were safely out of earshot. Today, Jim was wearing a pair of loose khaki pants held up with a worn leather belt and a tight white t-shirt that set off the burnished walnut of his late-summer tan. Mikey had found out that Jim had worked on a construction site all summer in the sun. He'd promptly made a note to add the image of Jim, working shirtless, slick with sweat and wearing a gleaming yellow construction helmet to his playlist of bedtime fantasies. "Look at how *buff* he is!"

"Jesus, Mikey," Wroxy said with disgust. "He looks like he should have 'Mattel' stamped on his ass. The guy is a dickhead of the first order. When did you get to be such a *fag*?"

"Since you forced me to come out to you, you bitch," he said in a low voice. He poked her with his index finger. "Remember? Besides," he added smugly, "I'm not saying that he's a nice person, just that he's incredibly hot."

"So be *gay* then. Don't be such a pathetically shallow *fag*. Do you remember who you're asking me to admire? This is the guy who calls me a 'devil-worshipping whore' and calls you a 'fudge packer.' This is the guy who smashed your CD player the day we met, remember?"

"In other words, we met because of Jim," Mikey said dreamily. "See? Something good came out of it."

"If you don't cut this crap out right now," Wroxy snapped, "you can fend for yourself this year without me watching your back. I'm sure as hell not going to sit around and listen to you carry on like a battered wife making excuses for the guy who beats the shit out of her every night."

"You take everything so seriously," Mikey said lightly. He held to his own idealized, romantic version of his feelings for Jim and he resented Wroxy's implication that there was something disturbing about his crush.

"Whatever." By now Wroxy was used to all of Mikey's moods, even the irritating ones that drove her mad with frustration. She looked at her watch.

"I have to run," she said. "I have some sort of meeting with the guidance counsellor that my mom set up. Apparently she's worried about the 'direction of my life' next year or something. I've got to go blow some sunshine up her ass for an hour or so. What do you have next?"

Mikey made a face. "Gym." He opened his locker door and placed the books he was carrying carefully back on the top shelf. Bending down, he pulled his gym bag from the bottom shelf.

"Ugh." They both hated gym with a passion. For Wroxy, it was a wasted hour out of her life when she was forced to play stupid games with girls she detested and avoided in every other instance. The fact that she was actually quite good at sports was something that she didn't admit to Mikey, who was spastically uncoordinated. Wroxy intuited that this was something that would diminish his already-tenuous sense of his own masculinity. Besides, she reasoned, it didn't matter. She hated the games whether she could play them or not, and resented this waste of an hour she could otherwise spend reading, writing, or drawing.

For Mikey, it was a nightmare hour when everything he was—or, more accurately, wasn't—became glaringly evident to everyone. From his early years of being unable to play the sports every other boy his age seemed to have learned by osmosis to his later years of not being strong enough to climb the rope with the other boys, of them being able to climb it with ease and of the gym teacher making the entire class wait for him to finish before they were allowed to play the sports they wanted to. Of being the last picked for every team, or accidentally scoring on his own team during a soccer game.

The shame in the locker room, when the other boys developed faster than he did, or the time that Dewey Verbinski waved his thick, hairy, uncut penis in Mikey's direction and asked him loudly if he wanted to suck it. The shame of seeing Jim Fields laughing at him while hot tears of shame coursed down his own cheeks as he covered himself with a bundle of his clothes, afraid to dress but too mortified to drop them lest it invite another torrent of abuse.

Yeah, gym class was hell. When Mikey graduated from high school, he was never going to step into another gymnasium in his life.

It was Jim Fields' idea, but Dewey wished he'd thought of it first.

Dewey was momentarily angry, an emotion so frequent with him that it passed like summer lightning. Besides, he would eventually claim that the idea was his, and Jim wouldn't challenge him. He never did.

They would nail the Childress faggot, nail him good, and get the senior year's reign of terror off to a good start. By next year at this time they would be out of school and Childress would be out of their grasp forever. Yeah, this was the year, all right. Best of all, this time they wouldn't have to touch him themselves. It was too cool.

The Childress faggot had slunk and moped around the edge of the shirts-and-skins basketball game like a girl no one wanted to fuck. Of course he couldn't play basketball. He couldn't play *anything*. Watching him stumble and mince and flail was an entertainment, one that usually had the whole gym class in stitches by halftime. It was better than television.

Childress's team captain, Shawn Curtis, had been forced to pick him—someone always was. Since Curtis was a natural athlete who played every sport superbly and was competitive as hell, he also wanted to win. Curtis solved the problem by keeping Childress off court for most of the game. His team had been skins, which was an added chance for Dewey and Jim to torment Mikey. Naked skin always hurt more when it was knocked to the ground and scraped, and it was easier to reach over and give Childress a hard titty-twist till he screamed and reached for his nipples. Of course Dewey and Jim—playing for shirts—were both disappointed that they were forced to hide their intimidating summer bulk under Auburn High athletic t-shirts, but they solved the problem by tying the shirts around their heads like turbans. The gym teacher, Mr. Sasseville, wasn't going to argue with Dewey Verbinski. He wasn't stupid.

After the game, the boys trooped into the locker room. They stripped off their clothes and strutted into the showers to hose off the afternoon's sweat. In short order the room echoed with adolescent male laughter. Soap-scented steam billowed out of the shower room into the locker room proper, and the air was clammy.

Dewey and Jim held back as the other guys jockeyed for space in the showers. They pretended to be deep in conversation, a ruse that was surprisingly effective for two boys whom no one would ever think of as having that capability for depth. When the coast was clear, Dewey stood guard while Jim, who was leaner and faster, vaulted across the locker room. Jim deftly unzipped the gym bag belonging to Shawn Curtis. In Dewey's opinion, Curtis was one of the stupider members of the Auburn High football team. He neither liked nor disliked Shawn Curtis, and that worked to his advantage. He would make a better weapon without either enmity or the loyalties owed to a comrade. Jim rummaged in the bag and pulled out one of Curtis's sweat-stained jockstraps. He made a disgusted face and waved his hand in front of his nose.

"Man!" Jim whined under his breath. "I don't want to be touching this thing! Fuck!" He held it at arm's length. It smelled ripe. The odour of other guys' ball sweat wasn't something Jim Fields cared for.

"Get over here, fuckstick!" Dewey hissed, gesturing furiously with one arm. "Hurry the fuck up before they get back! Come on, move it!"

Dewey crossed the floor to where Mikey Childress's gym bag lay open beside his locker. No one bothered with locks. *Stupid fuckers*, he thought darkly. He'd been stealing since he was nine and had more respect for people whose property he had to break into. People who left doors and windows open deserved what happened to them.

Jim sprinted over to where Dewey stood and placed the jockstrap in the Childress faggot's gym bag, tucking it under his gay little sweater and placing his yellow Discman on top. It occurred to him that the Childress faggot had managed to replace the Discman that Jim had smashed three years before. He briefly contemplated breaking this one, too, but concluded that it might warn Childress that something was up.

"Something's going to be 'up' all right, queer," Jim muttered under his breath. He smothered a laugh. The sight of the yellow Discman, however, continued to slight his sense of right and wrong. For good measure, he flipped open the lid and pulled out the CD. "Dew, look at this. He's listening to *Madonna*!"

"No shit," Dewey said distractedly. He gave a snort of all-purpose laughter just to show Jim that he'd acknowledged yet another example of Childress's faggotry, but his eye was on the shower-room door. "Leave it, asshole," Dewey snarled. "Curtis will be out in a second. Put the faggot's purse back where it was." Jim kicked the gym bag with his foot. He put the Madonna CD in the pocket of his track pants and reminded himself to take it out and snap it in half later.

Then the two of them hurried back to where they were sitting to watch the fireworks.

Shawn Curtis said, "What the *fuck*...?"

He slammed a ham-sized fist against the metal locker door. The sound echoed through the locker room like a gunshot. "All right, which one of you faggots took my jockstrap?" He smiled, not sure if the culprit would prove to be a teammate or close friend, in which case he didn't want to make too much of a scene, especially one that would make him look like an asshole later. On the other hand, if someone uncool was fucking with him, well, it would be their last fuck. Curtis looked around the room at the mute, nervous faces, most staring blankly. "Come on, guys. This isn't funny no more. I got class in ten minutes. Who took it?"

The only one who looked disinterested was Mikey Childress. Everyone in the room glanced automatically in his direction, more by rote than with malice. If anyone was going to fuck up or become the object of mockery or ridicule, it would be him. It wouldn't occur to any of the boys to look at anyone else. Lost in his own world in the way only those who are never included in locker room congenialities could be, Mikey busied himself inside his locker.

Curtis squinted his eyes, a look that was intimidating on the gridiron because it made him look a bit like a pit bull. Shawn

Curtis barely knew Mikey Childress, except to know what everyone knew—that he was a faggot. That was all someone like Curtis needed to know. The beginning of what to him was a disgusting suspicion was dawning.

"WHO STOLE MY FUCKING JOCK?"

At that moment, Mikey spun around as though he'd been shot in the back. The entire locker room was staring at him. In their eyes he saw a kaleidoscope of emotions, ranging from disbelief, to disgust, to relief that Curtis's fury wasn't focused on them.

Curtis walked toward him, menace in every stride. He extended his index finger, shoving it in Mikey's face. Mikey flinched and backed up.

This is not happening to me, he thought madly. *This is not happening to me here, not in front of these awful, awful people. Not here, not now. Please, God, I'll do anything.*

"Did you take my jockstrap, faggot?" Curtis said in a low, threatening voice. "Did you?"

"Your *what*? Jesus, no. Of *course* not."

And then, horribly, inevitably, the worst thing possible in this situation happened.

"Come on, Childress, admit it," Jim Fields said clearly. "Dew and I saw you. You'd better give it back." He smiled pityingly at Mikey, as though he knew what was coming and felt sorry for him. Mikey gaped open-mouthed at his idol. Shawn Curtis turned his pit bull gaze on Jim Fields, who met it the way equals do. Beside him, Dewey Verbinski smirked balefully at Mikey, not saying a word.

"What did you say, Fields?" Curtis took a step toward Jim Fields, his posture shifting away from the implicit violence offered by his stance toward Mikey. His shoulders relaxed, and he shifted from one foot to the other. Fields was cool.

"Curtis, I'm sorry, man," Jim said with ostentatious pity. "I didn't want to tell you here in front of everybody, but it's only, you know, fair in case this looks weird on you later."

"Weird on me? What the fuck are you talking about, Fields?"

Jim turned slowly to Mikey and nodded in his direction. This time he didn't even bother looking like he cared to pity him.

"Curtis, when you were in the shower room, Childress here went through your gym bag and took out your jock. Dew and I caught him sniffing it. He had this fuckin' smile on his face. Then," Jim added daringly, "he *licked* it."

Curtis looked between Childress, who seemed paralyzed, and Fields, who looked calmly at him with an indefinable expression on his face. Curtis laughed good-naturedly.

"You're full of shit, Fields. Now, where is it? I mean, if you're queer for me and you want to keep the jock, that's cool," he drawled. "But can I at least have it for the rest of the week?"

"Curtis," Dewey said in a flat, cold voice. "Fields isn't kidding. Check out the faggot's gym bag. It's in there. We saw him put it underneath some clothes. Your jock is in there. Just look."

Something in Dewey's voice gave Curtis pause. He strode toward Mikey, his large bare feet thudding against the concrete floor of the locker room. He pointed toward Mikey's gym bag and leaned into his face. Mikey stumbled backward, banging his hip painfully against the sharp edge of the locker.

"Open your bag, faggot," Curtis said. "Now. Open it."

Mikey stared at him. For one horrible moment he thought he was going to piss through the towel wrapped around his waist, flooding the bench and the floor, sealing his fate irrevocably and beyond any hope of redemption. He squeezed his bladder, willing it to containment.

Curtis reached past him roughly, pushing Mikey aside. Mikey smelled soap and deodorant. Curtis picked Mikey's gym bag up off the floor and unzipped the top. Curtis sat down heavily on the bench and began to rummage through the bag's contents.

Mikey was amazed that even in a situation as lethal as the one he was enduring, he was vaguely thrilled at his proximity to Shawn Curtis. He took stock of the cantaloupe-sized biceps, the thick slabs of back muscle, the skin flecked with a spray of acne that he'd heard was the result of steroids. By habit he noted all the ways in which Shawn Curtis was not like him, wondering with familiar confusion, as he did with most jocks, whether he wanted to *have* them, or *be* them.

And then, Armageddon.

"Oh ... my ... fucking ... God," Curtis gasped. "What the *fuck* ... ?"

In his hand, Shawn Curtis was holding his own frayed and faded jockstrap. He turned slowly to face Mikey, and his eyes were terrible.

As Mikey watched, a dark red flush appeared on the sides of Curtis's thick neck, spreading upward to his cheeks and forehead. The veins in his neck stood out like electric cables. Mikey clearly saw confusion, shock, dawning awareness, and embarrassment.

Then, rage.

The locker room was silent, and then Dewey Verbinski whistled.

"We told you, Curtis," he said. "We told you the faggot took your jock."

"Why didn't you stop him, man?" Curtis shouted. He took a step forward, a challenge implicit. But something cold and unflinching in Dewey's eyes gave him pause. "You let a *faggot* touch my stuff? What the fuck is wrong with you?"

"Hey," Dewey said slyly. He raised his hands in a gesture that was tinged with the exact amount of barely detectable innuendo to guarantee defensive outrage. "It was up to you to deal with it, dude. Would have told you, sure, but if you hadn't seen him do it, would you have believed me?"

Curtis stared dumbly at Dewey. Then he turned to Mikey. Almost as an afterthought, Curtis reached out and slapped him across the side of the head, open hand. The paste gemstone of his football ring bit into the flesh of Mikey's scalp. Purple stars exploded behind Mikey's eyes, and he crashed backward into the lockers. His towel fell off his waist, and he lay crumpled and nude on the cold, wet floor. Curtis leaned down and jabbed Mikey hard in the chest with his index finger.

"You're going to be so motherfucking sorry for this, Childress," he said softly, but loud enough that his voice carried through the entire locker room. "I promise you. You are going to wish you'd never been fucking born."

Curtis stood up and stalked over to his own locker. He dressed quickly, jamming his legs violently into his faded jeans. He grabbed his football jacket with the leather sleeves in one hand and his gym bag in the other. Looking neither right nor left, meeting no one's eye, he strode out of the room. The door slammed shut in his wake, moving the air.

The others, most of them already half-dressed, finished clothing themselves and left the room as the bell rang in the hallway outside, announcing the next period.

Dewey and Jim loped past the spot where Mikey lay stunned on the floor. His head throbbed where Curtis's football ring had cut him. Their eyes blazed with dark merriment. Jim pursed his lips and blew Mikey a kiss, fluttering his fingers in a gesture of ostentatious effeminacy. "Nice to see ya, wouldn't wanna be ya," he crooned. "Bye-bye, Childress. Have a *great* day!"

Ugly laughter trailed in their wake as they left. Mikey realized that he was crying again—and that he hated himself in that moment as much as he knew they hated him.

Wroxy took a deep drag on her cigarette and contemplated Mikey, who sat across from her in the booth. He looked, if possible, even more miserable and terrified than the morning he'd told her about finding the witches.

On one hand, Wroxy thought, hiding Shawn Curtis's jockstrap in Mikey's bag was the stupidest trick she'd ever heard of Jim and Dewey pulling. A tiny, dark, treacherous part of Wroxy's mind wondered how Mikey kept getting himself into these situations and if it was somehow not, at least in part, his fault. But the dominant, and much kinder, part of her pushed this cold question down. You just had to look at him, she thought. *No one deserves this, no one.* She wondered again, as she had on so many other occasions, how much Mikey could take before something snapped. She'd heard that gay kids committed suicide at a much higher rate than their straight peers. Though intellectually she understood exactly why this was, looking now at Mikey's shaking hands as he held the coffee mug, she understood it viscerally as well.

It was four o'clock in the afternoon, and they were sitting in a corner booth at the coffee shop next door to the Milton Mall. Mikey hadn't wanted to go to the mall itself. He was terrified of running into any of the guys from his gym class, especially Shawn Curtis.

Wroxy didn't tell him that she'd heard about the incident in her afternoon classes before Mikey had come to her after school, pale and shaken. Tina Mitterhaus and Gwen Horlick—who never spoke to Wroxy unless it was to call her names—had sidled up to her on the way into their last period social geography class.

"Wroxy, may I say just one thing to you?" Gwen's voice had been acidly sweet. "For your own good?" Behind her, Tina giggled. They looked at each other and pursed their glossy pink lips as though suppressing more laughter, as though between them, they held the funniest secret of all time.

"That's one thing already, Horlick," Wroxy had shot back. She knew Gwen hated her last name. She often talked about changing it, either herself or through marriage. Everyone knew she had a crush on Shawn Curtis. Wroxy had once caught her writing *Gwen Curtis* and *Gwen Horlick Curtis* and *Gwen Horlick-Curtis* in various signatures on the back of her English composition notebook. "And if it's from you," she added, "it likely isn't for my own good."

Unlike Mikey, Wroxy wasn't afraid of her peers and of wielding her sharp tongue like a whip when necessary. Generally they left Wroxy alone. Which was all the more reason why this entirely insecure overture from Gwen Horlick was so odd.

"Very funny, Wroxy," Gwen had replied smugly. "Haven't you heard? Your little gay boyfriend went too far this time. I'm worried about him, you know? Some people are really pissed at him. You know," she added with meaning, "*really* pissed. He should probably watch himself. You know, like not fall down any stairs or walk into any walls or nothing."

"What the fuck are you talking about, Horlick?" Wroxy snapped. She noted with some pleasure that Gwen flinched at the expletive as well as at Wroxy's continued use of her last name. "Are you on crack? What are you babbling about?"

"Well, you'd know more about *crack* then I would, you *whore*." Bright red spots flamed on Gwen's cheeks.

Wroxy leaned forward and laughed in Gwen's face. "At least my name isn't 'Whore-lick.' And it's never going to be 'Whore-lick-

Curtis.' Of course," Wroxy jeered, "neither is yours." She turned her back on Gwen and Tina and began to gather her things.

"We'll see if you're still laughing when your perverted queerboy gets what's coming to him," Gwen said behind her.

Wroxy turned just in time to see Tina elbow Gwen in the ribs, mouthing *Shut up!* as she did. Gwen stared at Wroxy with frank loathing, unable to maintain the saccharine façade she had essayed earlier. For her part, Wroxy had matched the loathing watt for watt.

"What did you say?" She took a menacing step toward Gwen, who flinched again but stood her ground. "What did you just say to me, Horlick?"

"Never mind, bitch," Gwen snapped. "You had your chance."

And that was the end of it. The girls had pivoted on their heels and swept past her. Wroxy had briefly contemplated grabbing a fistful of Gwen's hair as she passed and ripping it out at the root, but she thought better of it. She realized a fight this close to class would only lead to a suspension, and would attract much more attention than she wanted. Gwen and Tina went to the back of the classroom and sat in their accustomed seats surrounded by their friends.

Wroxy tried to concentrate on the lesson, but she was suddenly very afraid for Mikey. When she'd found him waiting for her outside the main doors of the school, standing as close as possible to the school buses, hands stuffed in his pockets, she'd hustled him off school property and into the coffee shop, where he'd told her the story while Wroxy had stared in disbelief.

The late afternoon fall sunlight slanted through the plate-glass windows. It was easy light, flattering, golden and pellucid, but Mikey still looked like shit run over twice.

Outside the windows, mothers with children safely in the back seats of their SUVs manoeuvred into the mall parking lot, expertly jockeying for the few remaining spaces. Groups of teenage girls, hair swinging in point-counterpoint to the sway of their newly full hips as they moved like a herd of painted gazelles through the lambent September afternoon, studiously ignoring the louche, slouching packs of teenage boys who trailed in their wake. They knew the boys would never be too far behind.

Wroxy glanced briefly at the pageant of middle-class normalcy, then looked away in barely perceptible disdain. The supercilious pride in being part of the movement of an ordinary life, one that excluded any and all that weren't ordinary, had a terrible cost, in her opinion.

And she was sitting across from that cost. Silently she again damned the Shawn Curtises, the Gwen Horlicks, and the Dewey Verbinskis of the world. And she especially damned Jim Fields.

"Do you want to stay over at my house tonight?" Wroxy offered. "We could tell your mother that we have a project. It'd be all right with my mom, I know. That way even if those guys came looking for you, they wouldn't find you."

"My mom would never let me," Mikey said. "She'd never let me stay at a girl's house overnight."

"I'm not 'a girl,' I'm your best friend. Your mother has known me for three years."

"Even still." He sighed. "No way would she ever let me."

"Your parents crack me up," Wroxy said with bitter humour. "On one hand, they're afraid you're not enough of a man, but on the other hand you're *too much* of a man to stay over at my house. Do they think you'd ravish me or something? Knock me up?"

Mikey smiled wanly, momentarily distracted. "What do you think I should do? Do you think I should tell my parents about this?" Even as he said it, Mikey was already dismissing bringing his parents into it. His mother wouldn't even be able to hear the word "jockstrap" without fainting, and he could imagine his father's face turning purple with embarrassment at the whole situation. Mikey knew full well that his father would blame him somehow for the altercation with Shawn Curtis, even if only for being such an easy target, as though being a source of discomfort for "normal" boys was provocation enough to warrant violence. Mikey had no doubt about whose side his father would come down on if he'd been one of the boys in the locker room this afternoon. He knew that men like his father were what most of these boys would grow up to become.

"Okay, let's look at this situation rationally," Wroxy said calmly, once again assuming the role of wise counsellor. "Do you think that

Shawn Curtis really believed it was you? I mean, I know he's not the sharpest knife in the drawer—even for a football player. But do you think he really believes you'd be stupid enough to steal his jockstrap in the middle of a locker room full of people?"

"He believes it." Mikey shivered. "It's so obvious that it was Dewey who did it. He planted the thing in my gym bag to embarrass Curtis on purpose. He wants something terrible to happen to me. He wants Curtis to beat me up. That's why he did it. Dewey hates me."

"Dewey and *Jim*," Wroxy corrected him sharply. "Goddamn it, get your head out of your ass, Childress. This crush of yours is going to kill you one of these days. They were in on it together. You know they were. They hate you. They *both* hate you."

Mikey sipped his cold coffee silently. He watched her over the rim of his cup.

Wroxy sighed. "Okay, so he believes it. Do you think he can be reasoned with?"

"Who, Dewey?" Mikey stared at her blankly. "What do you think?"

"No, not *Dewey!*" Wroxy practically shouted. "*Curtis!* If we went over to his house right now and talked to him, do you think he'd listen to reason? What if we told him what happened? That Dewey *and Jim* hid that revolting thing in your bag to get you into trouble?"

Mikey had never thought of his peers in terms of reason. The thought of going to Shawn Curtis's house and confronting him filled Mikey with dread. But he knew that he had fewer options than ever. All afternoon he'd felt their eyes on him. He'd heard whispers and muffled, incredulous laughter. When he'd looked up, he'd faced disgusted stares and mocking smiles. But unlike the mocking smiles he'd endured for most of his life, he'd sensed in these a malignant undercurrent of anticipation. For the most part, Dewey—and beautiful Jim—watched him lazily, both expressionless save for Dewey's signature half-smile that never touched his cold eyes.

"Do you know where Shawn Curtis lives?" Mikey asked. He was warming to the idea of taking the situation directly to the source. He hoped that perhaps, away from the crowd, Curtis might be more prepared to listen to reason. As usual, Wroxy was right on the money.

"No, but it shouldn't be too hard to find him in the book. That stupid twat Gwen Horlick is always talking about him. She says he has his own telephone number. Apparently she called it once but was too scared to talk when he picked up. Pathetic. All we need to do is look for a *Curtis, S* with the same address as another Curtis. The other one should be his parents. Does he live in Milton or Auburn?"

"Auburn, I think. I saw him outside St. Michael's once with his family. I think they live over in the Estates," Mikey said, naming an exclusive new subdivision being built north of town.

"All right, hold on." Wroxy got up and walked to the back of the coffee shop to the pay phones. She located the Milton-Campbellville-Auburn directory amid the jumble of regional phone books encased in hard black plastic, suspended on wires from the base of the pay phones. She opened it and riffled quickly through the dirty white pages, guiding her index finger down the column of names until she located *Curtis, S* on Blenheim Court in the Estates.

"Blenheim Court," she muttered disgustedly under her breath. "These people." Then louder to Mikey she said, "Found him. Let's go see what we can do."

"Shawn's busy right now," said the expensively dressed older woman who answered the door of the sprawling new mock-Tudor on Blenheim Court. The house sat on a field of dirt, the contractors not having yet had the time to lay down the sod for grass. Wroxy and Mikey deduced that the woman staring at them with ill-concealed disdain was Shawn's mother. "He can't come to the door. He's with his dad."

Mikey shuffled his feet. "I'm in his class," he said weakly. "My name is Mikey Childress. I just want to talk to him for a second. It won't take long, I promise."

The woman stiffened. Her eyes turned flinty as she stared at Mikey and Wroxy. When she spoke, her voice was arctic. "I know who you are. You have a hell of a lot of nerve to show up at our house and ask for my son."

"Look, Mrs. Curtis, he didn't do anything," Wroxy said. "That's the whole point. Your son's friends set Mikey up, and now he just wants to talk to him and settle this. Would you get him, please? Like we said, it will only take a couple of minutes."

"As *I* said, young lady, my son has nothing to say to your friend. Please get off our property at once." From behind the door Mikey heard the sound of muffled male voices. Mrs. Curtis half-turned toward them and said, "*I'm* handling this, Jeremy! Shawn, stay inside."

Mikey took a step forward and called out, "Shawn! I didn't do it! Please let me talk to you!"

"Go away!" Mrs. Curtis hissed, blocking the doorway. "Go back to where you came from! Get off our property or I'll call the police! Or your parents! You need to get some help, son. You're not normal!" She slammed the door in their faces. Mikey heard the bolt drawn on the other side.

Wroxy looked at him mutely and spread her hands in a gesture of resignation. "Can't say we didn't try, Mikey. We really should tell your parents about this before something happens."

"We can't," he said. "They won't believe I didn't steal it."

"Yes they will! I'll tell them, too! For God's sake, we need to tell *somebody* or they're going to kill you!"

"I'm already dead," Mikey said flatly. "I'm dead as shit."

That night, Mikey dreamed of swinging fists and broken bones. He dreamed of trying to dodge blows but being unable to. He dreamed of drowning in a warm red sea. He awoke gasping for air, his sheets drenched. Frantically he fumbled for the light switch, needed to see with his own eyes that his sheets were only soaked with sweat. Still, he touched his chest and side, feeling a phantom pain, looking for a wound, but there was none. His throat felt raw, as though he had been screaming.

Mikey listened to the sound of the sleeping house all around him.

"I'm alone," he whispered, if only to hear a sound, any sound, even his own voice. He didn't even think of Wroxy.

This time, Mikey didn't cry. He just hugged his pillow to his chest and tried to fall back to sleep with his bedroom light on.

They lay in wait for nearly two weeks. During that time, Mikey was left alone.

Later he would realize that it was likely deliberate, intended to establish distance. To Mikey, though, at the time, it was a period of blissful peace unlike any he could recall in high school. That in itself should have given him a sense of alarm but, forever optimistic, he dared to allow himself to imagine that Shawn Curtis and his friends had either forgotten about punishing him, or that Dewey Verbinski and Jim Fields had confessed their prank to Curtis, who, in turn, was keeping quiet about it out of embarrassment over how angry he'd gotten. In the alien, masculine world Mikey pictured these boys inhabiting, he imagined they settled these situations according to arcane rituals of fraternal bonding, like men. Stoically, privately.

"I think it's going to be okay," he told Wroxy happily as they sat on the grass of Rotary Park beside the millpond in Milton as the warm Indian summer sunlight faded from the sky. "I think they're over it."

Wroxy wasn't so sure. "Be careful," she said. "It's too early. Just watch your back."

Even as Wroxy said it, she was secretly, cautiously optimistic. She didn't want Mikey to lower his guard and start calling attention to himself, but at the same time she had sensed a loosening of the tension in the hallways and in the classroom. She'd cast a protection spell over Mikey on the day he'd told her about the incident. She was daring to believe the spell had been one of her more successful conjurations. When they parted, she told him that her powers were keeping him safe.

The September days were indeed achingly warm and sweet, but at night, the air turned cold. This classic early-autumn weather was coaxing from the leaves a foretaste of the glorious sourball colours that would burn like a low flame all through October and into November.

That night, Mikey put on a sweater and took his bicycle out for a ride, his first night ride since the one in August when he'd seen the witches. The terror of that night had receded in his memory, and he was more than prepared now to accept Wroxy's explanation of what he'd seen. He was sad about the goat—that part he knew he'd really seen—but there wasn't much he could do about it now. He inhaled the sweet night air as the wind blew his hair away from his forehead.

Mikey pedalled past the dark shop windows on Main Street. He turned left up Lilac Lane, passing the red brick Auburn Library. He zipped down dark streets, passing the high school, and circled the outskirts of town. He looked over toward the hulking stone shoulders of the escarpment. Beneath the wheels of his bicycle, the smooth paved road gave way to rumbling dirt. Above him, the bright September moon waxed in the night sky.

Mikey didn't notice the car tailing him with its lights off until it was much, much too late.

When the car careened toward him, tires screaming against the road, Mikey swerved to avoid getting hit. He lost his balance, and the bike veered sharply, then crashed into the ditch.

Agony sang through his shoulder as he felt sharp rock and gravel shear through the soft wool of the sweater, ripping the skin of his arms. The crossbar smashed into his solar plexus, knocking the air out of him. Gasping for breath and prone, he heard the car doors open, then slam shut. At dirt level, he saw five pairs of thick legs walk with measured steps to the place where he lay bleeding, face scratched and smudged with dirt. He looked up and saw Curtis, Dewey, Jim, and two others, older guys he'd seen around town but could only vaguely place. One of them swung a Louisville Slugger baseball bat, tapping it in almost absentminded rhythm against his thigh.

"We told you, you were going to wish you'd never been born, queerboy," Shawn Curtis said. His voice was slurred. Mikey caught the sharp, sour smack of stale whiskey on his breath.

They fell on him like a storm.

After the first blow, Mikey lost count.

He limped home, pushing his bicycle ahead of him when it became too painful to ride it, weaving slowly down the dark, pristine streets of Auburn. He didn't get to his house until nearly ten o'clock. If his parents had been home—his father was working late and his mother was at church—Mikey knew they would have been angry at him for being out so late, and he was only mildly comforted at the thought that if they had seen him, broken and dirty and bleeding, they would have felt bad for their anger.

Ultimately, though, it didn't make any difference. He could never tell his parents what had happened.

"You tell them you almost got hit by a car and fell off your bike," Shawn Curtis had said when the beating was finished. His breathing was stertorous and laboured. The whiskey hit Mikey like another slap when Curtis leaned in close, pushing his face into Mikey's. "You tell them you fell into a ditch and hurt yourself bad. You say one word about what happened here and you die, got it? You'll find out what happens to faggots in this town."

Mikey could only nod. The filthy jockstrap was still stuffed in his mouth. Before gagging him with it, they had taken turns urinating on it while Shawn Curtis held him down, pressing Mikey's face into the dirt.

"C'mon, let me use the bat," whined one of the guys Mikey didn't know. "C'mon, the little fuck will never tell. It's awesome, man. We used one on a queer in the city last summer. Shoulda heard him scream."

"Shut up, asshole." Dewey sounded regretful, like he wished he didn't have to be the voice of reason. "You wanna go to jail?"

"Yeah, shut up, asshole," Jim parroted loyally. "Dew is right. You wanna go to fuckin' *jail*?"

"I could fix it so no one would ever find this faggot ever again."

"Both of you *shut up!*" Shawn Curtis screamed. He grabbed Mikey by the front of his shirt with one hand, lifting him up off the road. With the other hand, he roughly snatched the piss-soaked jockstrap out of Mikey's mouth. He let go of Mikey's shirt and Mikey fell back hard on the ground. Curtis leaned in again. He thrust his index finger in Mikey's face. "Remember what I said, Childress. Not one word. And if you ever come near me again, your life won't be worth living, I swear to fucking God."

Mikey had nodded mutely. After one last hard, threatening stare, Curtis had stood up and walked back to the car. The others followed. Mikey heard the ignition and the car started to life. The last in the car was Jim Fields, who turned back slowly to face Mikey.

Jim smiled, almost playfully, then placed his finger on his lips and said, "Shhhhh." He winked, then climbed into the back seat.

As the car drove away Mikey tasted piss and dirt. And he tasted something new, something other than pain and sadness and loneliness and fear.

For the first time in his life, Mikey Childress tasted hate.

22

At home he peeled off his dirty, bloodstained clothes and placed them in a garbage bag. He examined his body in the mirror. The boys had been brilliantly efficient in their work. Although much of his body was black and blue, they had very cleverly left his face and neck alone. He could cover up his bruises with a turtleneck. Gym class would be another matter entirely, but he had no illusions that any of the other guys in his class would blow the whistle. *They likely all knew about it anyway*, he thought viciously. *They were all in on it.* Besides, he'd been told what to tell people. He'd fallen off his bicycle, remember? Clumsy, stupid wimpfuck that he was.

Mikey stepped into the shower and stood under the spray. The hot water hurt too badly, so he adjusted the temperature to a tepid cascade. He massaged shampoo into his scalp, barely noticing that the water ran brown with filth and then faintly pink with dried blood. He turned his face up to the spray and opened his mouth to rise the bitter aftertaste of urine from his tongue.

Mikey dried himself carefully, dressed in a long-sleeve sweat-shirt and sweatpants, then took three painkillers from his mother's medicine cabinet and washed them down with tap water. He lay down on his bed and closed his eyes, not to sleep but to try to calm the bedlam of thoughts in his head. Over and over Mikey replayed the assault in his mind, remembering every detail of Shawn Curtis's bellicose red face, his fists flying, finding purchase. In slow motion, he replayed Dewey Verbinski's vulpine pleasure as he punched Mikey's arms and shoulders hard. For once, Mikey noted, the supercilious half-smile was gone, the mask of control ripped away to reveal the emerging young monster within, whose capacity to inflict pain and suffering would someday be limitless. And he thought of Jim, beautiful Jim, taking his turn pissing on the jockstrap that Shawn Curtis shoved into his mouth while he gagged. He opened his eyes and looked up to where Jim's photograph was tacked up on the wall above his computer.

Wroxy was right. He hates me. He always did. All I ever wanted was to love him.

A rage unlike any he had ever felt suddenly engulfed Mikey. He sat bolt upright and swung his legs over the side of the bed. He crossed the floor to his desk and savagely ripped the photograph of Jim off the wall and tore it to pieces. He had a sudden, vivid impression of the goat whose throat he had seen slashed, but in his mind it was Jim's throat, not the animal's, from which the blood ran. He imagined Jim's naked, prone body, head nearly severed, being lifted up and pulled into the air.

And then he froze as the memory crashed into him full force.

"I *did* see it," Mikey said aloud. "It *did* happen. I didn't imagine it."

Wroxy had told him he had imagined everything, and he had believed her because he wanted to believe it. He wanted to feel safe, like he was living in a sane world. But he wasn't living in a sane world, and he wasn't safe. He would never be safe, not in a world where people like Shawn Curtis, Dewey Verbinski, and Jim Fields called the shots.

Well, change it then. Change your world. Change theirs.

Mikey turned his head sharply toward the door. The voice had been low and warm, and curiously familiar, each word solid and perfectly formed. But it was as if the words had been punched out of the air.

"Who's there?" he called out.

There was no one standing behind him. He stepped out of his bedroom and peered into the dark hallway. It was empty. He touched the side of his head, feeling a moment of vertigo, wondering if he had sustained a concussion and was now hearing voices.

Mikey sat down heavily on his bed and stared at the wall of books on witchcraft and demonology. He had read them all, had memorized entire sections. He thought of Wroxy's well-meaning charms and amulets, her incense and her meditation. A fat lot of good any of it had done for her—or even him, for that matter. She hadn't even believed him when he'd told her what he'd seen in the forest that night, which meant she had betrayed him. She was a fake, in her way, just like those other people.

But he had seen power that night, and whether or not anyone else in the world believed him, he knew that it was there to be used.

"Yes," he said. "I'll change their world all right."

Mikey typed "Witch+Milton+Ontario" into the window of his browser and pressed "Enter." The search engine produced 6,420 results, including announcements about a forthcoming Halloween pageant and the private sale of a used Ditch Witch 350 SX tractor plow. By the time he opened the twelfth page of listings, Mikey realized that there was going to be nothing useful on the Internet about the witches of the Niagara Escarpment, and even if there was, it couldn't rival what he already knew. He wondered idly if Wroxy had been lying to him, three years ago, when she'd said that there were stories "all over the Internet" about the coven.

Mikey deleted that page of listings and opened up a new window. He paused, then typed "revenge spell" into the browser window. This time, the search engine returned 1,420,000 results. Mikey groaned. He clicked on the first link and began to scroll through them. By one o'clock in the morning he had opened nearly three hundred links. Most were for generic broken-heart spells and seemed as though they had been written by teenage Goths in the throes of heartbreak. Even one titled "Ritual to Cause Pain to the One Who Made You Suffer" was primarily a visualization spell that involved staring at the photograph of an antagonist and sending him or her "bad energy."

An hour before dawn he clicked the arrow at the bottom of the screen one last time. The computer shuddered, then the screen refreshed itself. Mikey looked down at the screen as a flash of colour caught his attention. All of the websites listed on the screen appeared as blue hyperlinks, yet at the top of the screen he saw a line of red type. Instead of words, the title heading of the link was composed of runic symbols that reminded Mikey less of the ones he had seen in Wroxy's books on witchcraft and more like Cyrillic letters or samples of ancient Aramaic text he'd seen in history books and on television.

He stared at the link. There was no website address listed for the site.

This is impossible, Mikey thought. *If a website is listed with a search engine, it has to have a web address.* Mikey frowned, then clicked the "Refresh" icon on the toolbar.

The screen dissolved, then reassembled itself. The line of brilliant red type still glowed at the top of the listed web sites. He glanced up at the "search" box at the top of the screen. The words he had typed—"revenge spell"—were still in the box. There was still no website address. Puzzled, Mikey clicked the link. At the bottom of the screen appeared the familiar words "Website Found. Waiting for Reply." Then "Loading. Please Wait." Mikey waited.

The screen opened onto a red background against which appeared an inverted gold pentagram in a circle. Beneath the pentagram were the words *The Doorway. Enter Here.*

Mikey clicked the pentagram. The red background was replaced by a new screen. At its centre was an out-of-focus photograph, a landscape of hills and sky that looked vaguely familiar. Mikey suddenly felt very cold. He was looking at what appeared to be an antique photograph of the escarpment behind Milton and Auburn. More specifically, he recognized the slope of the hills and the basin of the meadow where he had seen the sacrifice. The photograph was framed in pulsing bars of light that marked it as yet another hyperlink. As though in a dream, Mikey dragged his mouse across the photograph and clicked it.

The lights in his room flickered, then went out.

The blue glow from the computer screen spilled out across the surface of Mikey's desk, illuminating his hands on the keyboard, but never touching the sudden yawning darkness at his back. He read the words that appeared on the screen.

Embrace Hate.

Mikey began to read the dense blocks of text, clicking the arrow button every time he reached the end of a page. He perused the diagrams; he read the earnest personal accounts of murder and sacrifice, of encounters with malefic demons that walked between worlds delivering unspeakable pain and suffering on behalf of those who had summoned them. As he read on, the revulsion he felt at the profane words and images was replaced by some cold knowing sense of their utter rightness. By dawn, he knew he had found what he was looking for.

When he reached the words of the revenge spell itself, Mikey did as he was told. He plucked a pen from the coffee mug on his desk and copied the words down in his own hand.

The next morning Mikey told his mother he thought he was coming down with something and ought to stay in bed. He sniffled conspicuously and pressed his tongue to the roof of his mouth when he spoke in order to sound like he had a sore throat. He'd fallen asleep at dawn and had the dark circles under his eyes that made a convincing case for the onset of illness.

Since Mikey was rarely sick, and even more rarely faked being sick to stay home (he always wanted to see Wroxy at school, and sometimes even entertained the conceit that *he* looked out for *her*), Donna believed him. Mikey was careful to wear his sweats so as not to alert her to the bruises, not that Donna noticed much of anything at seven a.m. when she was getting ready for work. She rubbed her eyes irritably, her hands fumbling around the kitchen counter as she looked for her coffee cup. His father had left the house half an hour earlier.

"Were you out riding around in the cold again, Mikey?" Donna demanded. "When are you going to get some sense? You know how the weather is this time of year. Warm all day, then . . . *pow!*"

"A lot of kids are coming down with something, Mom," he said. "It tends to only last a couple of days, but it wipes them out. I really feel like crap. If it's okay with you, I'm just going to go back to bed."

"Okay honey," she said absently. "There's juice in the fridge and there's some soup in the bowl with the plastic lid. I think it's still good. Call me at work if it gets worse. I don't think there's ice cream, but I'll try and bring some home with me when I get off tonight. Remember, I have choir practice and your dad has that farewell party for his supervisor at the plant. We won't be home till very, very late. Rest, okay? We don't want you missing too much school this early in the year."

"Okay, Mom. I'll probably just go to bed and stay there."

He lay in bed staring at the ceiling even after his mother popped into his bedroom to say goodbye. Only when he heard her car pulling out of the driveway did he throw back the covers and walk to the window. He looked up into the sky where the waxing moon had gone down only a few hours before. It would be full in a few days. Mikey smiled to himself thinking of it. He crossed to his desk and reached for the piece of yellow foolscap on which he had written the night before and looked down at his notes. Mikey had drawn a crude replica of the diagram he'd found there. The website had provided phonetic spelling for the words of incantation, though it neglected to identify the language of origin.

Mikey wondered idly where he was going to find a cat, and how best to kill it.

24

Wroxy phoned several times during the next week. Mikey let the machine take the calls during the day. His mother told him "that girl" was clogging up the answering machine with her plaintive calls asking how he was doing. Donna was surprised when Mikey told her to please answer the phone the next time Wroxy called, and tell her that he was sick and not up to talking or visitors. This, Mikey knew, his mother would relish. Donna had never made much of an attempt to hide her profound dislike of Wroxy Miller, whom she considered a bad influence on Mikey.

Each evening Mikey watched as the September moon climbed the night sky outside his bedroom window, growing gibbous and ever brighter, even as the cruel black bruises on his body yellowed and faded from sight. He consulted his lunar calendar and saw that the moon would reach the zenith of its fullness on Sunday night. The irony of what he was planning on what Donna never failed to refer to as "the Lord's night" filled him with both dark pleasure and an odd sense of sacrilegious dread.

On Thursday night his parents called him into the living room and asked him to sit down. Both looked serious, and for a moment Mikey thought that somehow his parents had stumbled across the piece of yellow paper locked in the top drawer of his desk.

"Mikey, your dad and I have some sad news," Donna said. It looked as though she'd been crying. Her eyes were puffy and her nose was red. "Please brace yourself. It's about your Nana."

"Mom, what's wrong?"

"Just listen, and your mother and I will tell you," his father said brusquely. "Just keep quiet, Michael, please."

Mikey said nothing. He looked from his father to his mother, then back again. He barely knew his grandmother, Rose, who lived on the border of Windsor and Detroit. His father wouldn't have Nana Rose in the house for reasons Mikey had never really understood, though he'd guessed it was another sore spot in his parents' marriage.

"Your grandmother, Nana Rose, has had a heart attack," Donna said in a wavering voice. "It's serious. She isn't expected to live past the weekend." She broke into fresh sobs and reached for a tissue and blew her nose loudly. This seemed to irritate his father, who scowled at Mikey.

"Your mother needs to go to Windsor to be with her," his father said. "Your grandmother has apparently asked to see both of us before she passes on." His mouth tightened. "I can't imagine why, but apparently this is important to her. It's clearly important to your mother that we both travel to your grandmother's . . . to her *deathbed*, even thought it means that I'll have to miss three days of overtime during our busiest time." His father glared at his mother, then looked away.

"Larry, please. She's my *mother*." Donna composed herself, then went on. "What your father and I want to know, Mikey, is whether you'd be all right for a few days by yourself? It's almost the weekend and there's plenty of food in the fridge. You've been sick, so it might be a good idea for you to keep resting until school on Monday. If we left for Windsor tomorrow morning, we'd be home on Monday night."

Mikey steeled himself not to reveal the overwhelming sense of relief and euphoria that threatened to swamp his composure. He adopted what he hoped was an expression of sadness mixed with bravery.

"Yeah, Mom," he said. "Not a problem. I'll be fine. You and Dad just do what you have to do. Don't worry about me. And tell Nana I love her."

"I will, Mikey," Donna said, patting his knee. "You're a good boy."

"No parties," his father said without a hint of irony. Then, contemptuously, "I guess parties are the one thing we don't have to worry about with you, are they, Mikey?"

His parents left the next morning before the sun came up. His mother left him instructions on how to microwave the leftovers in the fridge, and a twenty-dollar bill. They took his father's car. Mikey was relieved to see his mother's Honda in the garage.

Wroxy called four more times, then left one last angry message: "Mikey, this is Wroxy. I don't know what's up with you, or why you don't call me back, but I'm beginning to think you're mad at me for some reason." Her voice sounded hollow and bewildered, and Mikey felt a twinge of guilt for the sadness he heard. "Since I don't know what it is, and since you don't seem to have the decency to call me up and tell me so we can fix it, I'm beginning to wonder what this friendship of ours has been worth all these years. It's Saturday night. I'm home. If you don't call me before Monday . . . well, I don't know what. Okay, call me. Bye."

Mikey pressed the "Erase" button on the answering machine, then pressed it again, deleting all her messages.

On Sunday Mikey spent all day inside. At dusk he dressed in dark clothes and shoes and went out to the garage. Rummaging through the drawers in his father's workshop, he located a pair of thick leather gloves, which he placed inside his knapsack along with a can of tuna, a can opener, a kitchen knife, a box of salt, some matches, and a thick canvas sack that had once held a sleeping bag.

In the front zippered compartment of the knapsack was as sheet of yellow paper folded over twice. He patted the bag to make sure it was there. When he felt it, he reached through the open window and placed the knapsack on the floor beside the passenger seat of his mother's car.

Then he opened the car door, slid in behind the wheel, and went hunting.

25

Mikey found the cat near the entrance to the dump where it had been foraging for rats. He opened the can of tuna and crouched down into what he hoped was an unthreatening position. "Here, kitty," he crooned, tapping the can. "Come and have some nice fish."

The cat had taken some coaxing, but after a few minutes the smell of the open can of tuna proved irresistible. It was clearly used to people, likely a family pet judging by the way it came to him once it was convinced he meant it no harm. It licked its lips and began to nibble at the tuna.

Mikey fought the urge to stroke it before he jammed the canvas bag down over its head, flipping it backwards inside the bag and closing up the opening. He found himself in awe of the cat's strength as it fought inside the bag. His stomach churned as unexpected remorse crashed over him. It had been one thing to read about this on the website in context as he planned his revenge. It was something else entirely to hear the terrible sounds of rage and terror coming from inside the bag as the cat thrashed and rocked inside.

"Shut up," Mikey pleaded softly. "Just shut up. Stop screaming. I'm sorry, cat. I'm so, so sorry. It'll be okay. *Shhhhh.*"

Mikey opened the trunk and placed the bag on the floor as gently as he could. Then he closed it. Above him, the September moon hung full and fat in the night sky. He wiped his eyes, took a deep breath, and then climbed back into the car. He started the engine again and began to climb the roads that would take him to the highest point of the escarpment.

Mikey drove for twenty minutes till he reached his destination.

He pulled into a clearing and turned off the ignition. His legs trembled as he stepped out of the car and listened. The silence was broken only by the sound of the wind in the trees and the occasional scream of a night bird.

He reached for the knapsack and stepped farther into the clearing.

Mikey looked up again and checked the position of the moon in relation to where he was standing. Pouring salt from the box, he drew two concentric circles on the ground, one seven feet in diameter, one fourteen feet. With a stick he drew several crude symbols inside both circles. Shivering, he moved quickly, gathering up some dry wood into a pile at the centre of the inner circle, and built a small fire. When he was sure the fire was burning strongly, he walked slowly back to the car and opened the trunk. The cat was making low growling sounds inside the bag, but had stopped thrashing. Gingerly he reached over and picked up the bag. Instantly the cat began to fight for its life again. Mikey walked back over to the circles of salt and placed the bag outside the inner circle. He unzipped the front of the knapsack and withdrew the paper with the spell on it. His lips moved as he scanned the paper, checking that everything was as he had copied it down.

Mikey stripped off his clothes. He was suddenly conscious of the terrible cold, which reminded him of the cold that night behind the boulder, overlooking the meadow. He stepped closer to the fire but it did little to warm him. He reached back into the knapsack and withdrew the heavy leather gloves and the kitchen knife, laying them down on the forest floor beside the fire. The instructions had been quite specific: the cat's throat would have to be cut, the blade drawn from right to left. Mikey took another deep breath, then put on the heavy leather gloves. He held the kitchen knife tightly in his right hand. He walked over to the bag and began to untie the cords that held the opening closed.

The cat lurched halfway out of the confines of the bag before Mikey grabbed it and tried to hold it in place. It hissed, its eyes wild with terror. Mikey screamed as the cat's claws raked across his bare chest. Blood spurted from the line of deep scratches that burned like fire. He'd never known such pain. Frantically he forced the cat's head back into the sack, pushing down as it sank its teeth into the thick leather gloves. Its claws slashed at Mikey's exposed arms and hands as he wrestled the bag shut, tying the top. He threw the bag on the ground, panting.

Mikey was abruptly consumed by black fury. In his mind, the pain of the cat's attack merged with the pain of his beating the previous week, and with the entire litany of agonies and humiliations throughout the years that had led him to this point.

Roughly he picked up the bag and threw it into the centre of the inner circle. He knew he couldn't cut the cat's throat, but the fucking thing would die now, that's for sure.

Mikey reached for a large, heavy rock. With a grunt, he brought it crashing down on the cat's head inside the bag. He heard a sickening crunch, then he struck again. The bag turned red beneath the blows. It shook once, then it was still.

He stared down at the bag. Breathing heavily, he picked it up and stepped into the inner circle. He knelt down and reached for the piece of yellow paper and began to read aloud the phonetically spelled incantation he'd written there. When he finished, he opened the bag and dumped the cat's mangled body at his feet. He forced himself to reach down and dip his fingers in its blood. On his chest he drew the symbol he'd copied onto the yellow paper. He bent down and picked up the kitchen knife again. Gritting his teeth, he cut a deep diagonal line across the centre of his left palm. The pain was incandescent. Mikey cried out as blood rose from the lips of the cut and flowed swiftly down his wrist. Blindly he stumbled over to where he had drawn the symbols in the dirt and let the blood from the wound on his hand spill onto the ground, covering the runes.

Then Mikey knelt. He closed his eyes and waited.

"Come to me," he whispered, using the permitted English words of the spell. His hand throbbed. "Come to me and do my bidding. Be my hammer."

Mikey waited in silence for several long minutes. And waited several more. He dared to look up into the air above him. No face had appeared in the smoke from his fire. No fingers reached down toward him from any cloud.

"Come to me!" he cried desperately. "Come to me! Do my bidding! Be my hammer!"

The first of the raindrops hit his face. The moon was obscured now by thick black clouds. Mikey flinched as the rain began to lash his naked body in earnest. Before the fire hissed out, Mikey caught sight of the pathetic tangle of wet fur, blood, and brain matter that had been the cat he'd killed. The rain fell heavier and heavier, becoming a torrential downpour. He heard the rumble of distant thunder, and lighting flashed in the distance.

"Come to me!" Mikey screamed, jumping up. *"Do my bidding! Be my hammer! You promised, goddamnit! Look at what I did for you!"*

The rain came like a waterfall. Gasping in shock beneath the frigid cloudburst, Mikey dressed in his soaking wet clothes in the dark. He ran for the car and opened the passenger-side door. By the interior light he located the knife and the leather gloves on the ground. The rain was already forming puddles near the circles he had drawn in salt, and was washing them away. He threw one more agonized look at the cat's mangled body, then doubled over in guilt.

Mikey climbed into the Honda and turned the key in the ignition. He revved the engine, tossing mud up into the air as the car peeled out of the clearing and onto the road back to Auburn. He glanced down at the dashboard clock. It was one o'clock in the morning on the last day of September—or rather, the first day of October— and he had just bashed out the brains of an innocent, defenseless animal in order to cast a spell he'd found on the Internet to make the bullies in town suffer for having hurt him.

Mikey felt he would vomit. He pulled the car to the side of the road and leaned out of the driver's side door just as his stomach began to heave.

All of this for nothing, he thought sickly, retching into the mud. *I killed a living thing for nothing. Yeah, I'm a real sorcerer, aren't I? I am Mikey Childress. Fear me. Christ almighty, what have I turned into?*

On the ride home it occurred to him that the best thing to do would be to drive off one of the cliffs and crash his mother's car into a ravine. It would solve a lot of problems. At the same time, he suspected, he probably didn't even have the courage for that.

ctober

September
August
July
June
May
April

The first day of October dawned crisp and brilliant in Auburn, as though the rain the night before had washed the landscape clean. Many of the townspeople had been woken by the storm, but most had simply turned over on their pillows and returned to sleep, soothed by the patter of raindrops on their roofs and windows. Although the temperature would climb by noon, early risers saw their breath as they retrieved newspapers from front porches or locked their houses before making their way to their cars. The warm days and cold nights of September's final week had set off a dazzling pyrotechnic display of vivid autumn colours in the leaves of the trees lining the streets, and the escarpment hills surrounding the town burned with cold fire in deep hues of yellow, orange, and red.

Mikey woke from his nightmares to bright sunlight stealing between the curtains of his room. His first thought was of the dead cat, and he felt his chest contract with grief and terrible guilt. He looked down at his bandaged hand. The bleeding must have stopped during the night because the bandage had dried to the colour of clay. He flexed his fingers gingerly but felt only mild discomfort. He unwound the bandage carefully. When he reached the final level of the binding, he tugged gently where the cotton was fused to the deep, ugly wound so as not to dislodge any scabbing. Feeling nothing, he tugged harder, then ripped the bandage off. He winced, anticipating a torrent of fresh, dark blood.

The bandage came away easily from the wound. The place where the knife had bitten into the soft flesh of his palm was smeared with dried blood, but instead of the ragged strip of severed flesh he'd seen the night before, there was a faded pink line of healing skin covered with a scab. He turned his hand over and looked at his fingers. The place where the cat had scratched him was unblemished and smooth in the morning light.

Feeling light-headed, Mikey slowly walked into the bathroom and stood in front of the mirror. He pulled his t-shirt over his head and stared at his pale, naked chest. During the night, blood had seeped from the scratches and smeared the skin in a crisscross pattern, but when he touched the place where the scratches would have been, the skin was unmarked, showing no trace of a wound. For several long minutes, Mikey stood in front of the mirror, staring stupidly at his own reflection, trying to make sense of what he was seeing. His thoughts were cloudy and torpid, as though he were still asleep. He turned away from the mirror, reached over and turned on the shower. Testing the water temperature with his hand, he pulled off his boxer shorts and stepped under the spray, letting the water run off the back of his cut hand, protecting the palm. He flexed the fingers again, feeling only the vaguest ache near the wound. He reached over and turned the hot water off. The stream of water ran cold. He forced himself to stand under the icy blast until his skin turned bluish and he began to shiver. Then Mikey turned the water off and stepped out onto the bath mat. He dried himself briskly with a towel until he felt warm again.

Mikey taped a large Band-Aid over the cut on his palm, which now seemed even less raw than it had been before the shower. His rational mind told him that the speed of this healing was impossible, but the practical convenience of having one less thing to explain to his parents overrode any disturbing questions that his mind whispered to him.

He looked down into the wastepaper basket in his bedroom, where a yard-long blood-soaked cotton bandage lay like a dead snake amid the paper and debris. Carefully he retrieved the bloody wrapping from the wastepaper basket and stuffed it into an empty manila envelope lying on his desk. He stapled the envelope shut as a final security measure, then shoved it to the bottom of the basket, covering it with paper. In the unlikely event that his mother came to empty the trash when she and his father returned from Windsor, she wouldn't take note of it.

He dressed quickly and went into the kitchen. The answering machine light was blinking. He pressed the button and waited. There was one message: his mother telling him that she and his father would be home late tonight, and not to wait up. Mikey, who had never felt less like seeing his parents, or anyone else, sighed with relief.

He had left half a pot of cold coffee in the coffee machine on Sunday morning. Mikey poured himself half a cup and gulped it down, nearly gagging at the bitter taste. But it served its purpose. As he gathered up his books and stepped outside into the cool October morning, his head was clear and he was fully awake.

The walk to school was blissfully uneventful. The residential section of Auburn was usually full of teenagers on their way to school at that hour, but Mikey encountered no one as he hurried down Webster Avenue toward the interlocking streets that led to Auburn High School. The books in his knapsack felt sharp and heavy against his back as he hurried along with his head down.

Wroxy was waiting for him just off the school property, nervously puffing on a cigarette. When she saw him, she dropped it to the pavement and ground it out.

"Mikey, where have you been?" Wroxy's voice was urgent. "What's wrong with you? I've been calling you for days. I've been worried sick."

He shrugged. "I'm sorry. I guess I just haven't felt like talking to anyone. I've been dealing with some shit, and I didn't want to get you involved. It's okay now, though."

"*Involved*?" she nearly shouted. "I'm your best friend! I'm already *involved*, wouldn't you say? You disappear for a week, you don't even call to tell me if you're alive or dead, and when I go over to your house, your fucking mother tells me that you're too sick to come to the door. And you and I both know she doesn't like me, so don't tell me that isn't part of why she didn't let me in to see for myself. What the hell is going down here?"

"Look, Wroxy, I'm really sorry about this. I really was sick, and I just didn't want to talk to anyone. Not even to you," Mikey added, remembering the negative thoughts he'd had about her during the past week. The concern and pain in her face struck him like a blow.

"What about these rumours I've been hearing?" she asked.

"Rumours?"

"Don't play stupid with me, Childress. I've been hearing rumours that you got the shit beaten out of you a few days ago, but everyone is being very cagey about it, and no one will mention any names. Did something happen? Is that why you were ducking school? Did somebody hurt you? You fucking tell me, and right now."

Before Mikey could answer, the nine o'clock bell rang. Scattered groups of straggling students hurried past them through the main doors. Mikey stared mutely into Wroxy's face and was moved by what he saw there. She was paler than usual and looked as though she hadn't slept well. There were bluish-purple smudges beneath her eyes that even thick makeup couldn't cover. He wondered once again, as he had on so many previous occasions, whether he and Wroxy had some sort of psychic bond that would have allowed her to share some of his own pain without even knowing it.

The sheer awfulness of the night before rose up in him. In the face of Wroxy's concern and obvious love, it threatened to drown him. His eyes blurred, and he bit down hard on his bottom lip so as not to cry.

Wroxy saw this and winced. She reached out her hand as if to touch his shoulder. Mikey flinched. "Look," he said tentatively. "Let's talk about this at lunch, okay? I don't want to get into it now. It's too complicated. All right?"

"All right." Wroxy sighed. "I can't make you talk to me. All I can do is ask you to remember how long we've been friends. You owe me that at least."

"Yeah. I owe you that at least."

"You know what?" Wroxy said. She looked miserable. "I'm going to bail on morning classes. If any of the teachers ask you, tell them I had a dentist appointment or something."

"Where are you going?"

"I don't know. Around. It doesn't really matter, does it?"

Mikey shook his head.

"I don't think I'd be able to concentrate very well. You think about what I said, and we'll talk at lunch. I'll meet you right here."

As Mikey entered the school, Wroxy hurried across the parking lot toward the street. She couldn't remember a moment when she felt further from him.

27

Mikey was lost in guilty thoughts about Wroxy when the new boy walked through the door of his homeroom class. His first impression was that the boy—if one could even call him that, since nothing about him remotely suggested callow vulnerability, or the tentativeness of a teenage male scenting unfamiliar territory—must be an adult, perhaps a young substitute teacher.

But no, there was Mrs. Wood, his homeroom teacher, sitting at her desk leafing quizzically through a folder full of papers that had arrived from the principal's office.

Unable not to stare, Mikey took in the square jaw, the thick, close-cropped white-blond hair. He guessed the boy's height to be six feet, maybe taller. He wore a black leather biker jacket over a plain red t-shirt. The wallet in the back pocket of his faded Levis was attached to a length of chain clipped to a black leather belt that enclosed his narrow waist. Lowering his eyes, Mikey saw that the boy wore heavy black boots, the cracked leather polished to a high shine.

When he looked up again, the boy was walking directly toward him. Mikey's eyes widened. In that instant, the boy met his gaze directly and smiled down at him.

"Hey," the boy said, extending his hand. His voice was a man's voice, not a boy's, deep and mellifluous, with no scratchy adolescent breakage. "I'm Adrian. And you are . . . ?"

There were several heavy silver bracelets encircling his wrist. Mikey gaped at the proffered hand as though he had never been asked to shake one in his life. He looked up at Adrian's face to see if there was any mockery there, if he had mistaken Mikey for someone else, and if there was a punchline forthcoming. Adrian met Mikey's quizzical stare with a gaze that was full and blue and warm. Mikey saw that his eyelashes were thick and dark, darker than he would have imagined against such white-blond colouring. Adrian looked German or Swedish. Or, at least, the way Mikey imagined Germans and Swedes looked based on movies he had seen.

Adrian half-smiled, then reached down to where Mikey's hand sat limply on his desk and grasped it gently, raising it to the shaking position. He squeezed it once, firmly. Mikey sensed enormous strength in Adrian's grip, but strength held under control for his benefit. In that second, all thoughts of witches, black magic, dead cats, bullies, or loneliness were driven from his mind.

"I'm Mikey. My name is Mikey Childress."

Mikey was suddenly aware that the entire classroom had gone silent. Across the aisle from where he sat, Tina Mitterhaus and Gwen Horlick were whispering to each other as they stared at him and Adrian. But instead of the derisive smirks that usually accompanied their whispers, they appeared unable to look away from Adrian. Mikey saw Gwen lick her lips.

Farther down the row Shawn Curtis seemed to be taking Adrian's measure as well.

At first Mikey thought it might be fear he saw in Curtis's eyes, but then he realized it was the sizing up of a potential adversary, the way boxers did in the ring before a match. In any case, whatever he saw there clearly gave him pause.

"Anybody sitting here?" Adrian said. He indicated the seat next to Mikey with a sideways glance. The seat was occupied by a thick-set hockey player named Chad Smith, whom Mikey barely knew, a buddy of Dewey and Jim's, though not one of his regular torment-ors. Adrian didn't look at Chad when he asked the question.

"Yeah, asshole," Chad said. "*I'm* sitting here. Are you blind? This is my seat."

"Not anymore it isn't," Adrian said softly. He turned away from Mikey and gave Chad his full attention. "Find another seat."

"Excuse me?"

"You heard me," Adrian said, and this time there was an edge to his voice that thrilled Mikey. "I told you to move." He leaned down and moved his face inches from Chad's face, placing both of his forearms on the hockey player's desk. "Was there some part of that you didn't understand?" For an impossibly long and challenging second, the two young men stared into each other's eyes.

Chad dropped his gaze first. He muttered something under his breath and gathered up his books, then stood up and walked to the back of the classroom where there was an empty desk next to Dewey Verbinski. Mikey dared to turn his head to follow Chad's progress to the back of the class. He saw that both Dewey and Jim were staring in disbelief as Chad made his way between the two rows of desks. He sat down heavily next to Dewey, refusing to look left or right.

Adrian slid gracefully into the empty seat next to Mikey and winked at him. He leaned back in the chair and put both hands behind his head. When he said, "You and I are going to be great friends, I can tell," Mikey's world seemed to tilt and go white at the edges.

"People, I'd like to introduce Adrian Johnson," Mrs. Wood said, looking up from the folder in front of her. "Adrian has transferred to our school from—" She paused and looked down again. "Connecticut." She smiled brightly. "Adrian, what brings you all the way to Auburn, Ontario for your senior year?"

"My father is from here," Adrian said with another dazzling smile at Mrs. Wood, who blushed under his direct gaze. "He sent me on ahead. He'll be moving back here at the end of the month. Until then, I'm on my own."

"Well, we're very glad to have you. Auburn is a lovely town. You'll be making friends in no time."

"Oh, I'm already making friends, ma'am," Adrian said with another sideways grin in Mikey's direction.

28

What happened in the cafeteria at lunch was something that Mikey—even in his wildest romantic daydreams or revenge fantasies—would never have dared to conjure.

One minute Dewey Verbinski was standing in front of him and Adrian in the lunch line making a comment about ass bandits and boyfriends; in the next, Dewey had been pitched halfway across the lunchroom. He lay sprawled on the floor with his hands pressed to his face. Blood gushed through the protective interlock of his fingers, and the gurgling whine that issued from behind his hands sounded like he might be drowning in his own blood. Someone had shouted *Whoa!* as Dewey crashed into a grouping of empty chairs, sending nearby trays and plates smashing against the concrete floor. The sound of Adrian's fist connecting with Dewey's face had been sharp and clear.

Mikey gaped. Adrian didn't even look back.

"Where do you want to sit, Mikey Childress?" Adrian's strong voice carried through the now-silent cafeteria. He placed his hand in the middle of Mikey's back and propelled him gently forward. "Do you have a favourite seat?"

"I usually eat outside," Mikey said. His throat felt dry. "I don't usually like it in here."

"Well, we can go outside if you like. Whatever you want. I don't think your buddy back there is going to bother you for a while, so if you want to sit in here, that would be cool, too. I think I broke his nose." Adrian's laugh was genial. "What an asshole. Is he usually like that?"

"No," Mikey said darkly. "He's usually much worse."

Adrian looked nonplussed. "So, inside or outside?"

"Let's go outside," Mikey breathed.

In the noon sunlight, Adrian and Mikey sat beneath a maple tree that was already losing its leaves. A gust of wind sent a handful scattering into the air, cascading down over them as they sat on the grass.

"Can I ask you a question?" Mikey said.

"Sure." Adrian bit into an apple. He'd taken off his leather jacket and laid it on the ground beside him. Mikey caught a whiff of the leather as the sun baked into it. Adrian's pale arms were corded with sinew, and Mikey watched rapt as they flexed easily, even in the simple gesture of raising an apple to his lips.

"Why did you do all this for me today? I mean, you didn't have to, you know. No one has ever hit Dewey Verbinski before, and no one has ever stuck up for me." Mikey suddenly thought of Wroxy and felt another spasm of guilt, which vanished as he stared into Adrian's blue yes. "You could be friends with anyone here. Why are you having lunch with me, of all people?"

Adrian shrugged. "I think you're cool. I like you. I hate it when these people pick on you."

"You hate it?" Mikey was puzzled. "You've never seen it before. This is your first day at school."

"It makes me angry to see bullies beat up on people who can't defend themselves. I'm a bit of a defender. " Adrian smiled. "I'm a bit of an avenging angel, to be honest. Always have been."

Mikey persisted. "But why me?"

"You and I are a lot alike," Adrian said. His fingers grazed Mikey's hand lightly. "I like you a lot. And if anyone wants to start shit with you anymore, they can take it up with me first. I'll protect you," he added playfully. "Don't worry."

"Hey," Wroxy said. She had come up behind them but Mikey hadn't heard her approach. He turned around. She stood with her weight shifted to one side. Idly, she tapped her foot on the ground. "What happened to you? I waited by the front door for half an hour." She looked down at his tray and her eyes widened. "You went into the cafeteria? We were supposed to meet and talk!"

"Oh, hey, Wroxy!" Mikey said excitedly. "This is Adrian Johnson. He's new. Adrian, this is my best friend Wroxy."

"Hello, Wroxy, "Adrian said easily. "Any friend of Mikey's is a friend of mine."

"Yeah, whatever, dude. I don't even know you. We're not friends yet, and if you just met Mikey, you're not his friend yet, either."

"Wroxy, what the *fuck*?" Mikey was shocked. "That's so rude. I can't believe you said that. I'm so sorry, Adrian, she didn't mean it."

"Don't apologize for me, Mikey," she said coolly. "Okay? You and I were supposed to meet for lunch and talk about what's been going on with you lately, and instead I find you here on the grass with a perfect stranger. No offence—what did you say your name was? Adam? It's just that Mikey and I have a long history here, and we have some business."

"No offence taken, Wroxy. And it's Adrian, not Adam." He stood up and brushed off his jacket before casually slipping it on. "Look," he said to Mikey, "if you two have things to talk about, I'll catch up with you later. I'm going to go have a smoke behind the maintenance shed. Take care, Mikey," he said with a private smile. "I'll look for you in a bit. If anyone gives you any trouble over what happened in the cafeteria, let me know, okay?"

Wroxy watched Adrian lope across the football field behind the school toward the outbuildings on the edge of the property. "You want to tell me what that was about?" In spite of herself, her eyes were drawn to Adrian's strong, thick legs in the blue denim, the way the sunlight gleamed off his leather jacket, and the breadth of the shoulders it encased like black armour. Wroxy felt a warmth and dampness building inside her. She turned away from Mikey so he couldn't read the unfamiliar desire in her face.

"Isn't he *gorgeous*?" Mikey sighed. His eyes, too, were riveted on Adrian's retreating figure. "He's *exactly* my type. Did you see his body? Big, but not too big. And that leather jacket, oh my God. He told me he's nineteen. He's from the States—Connecticut, I think, or Colorado. One of those places that starts with a *C*. Can you believe it? He moved from the *States* to come *here*! What are the odds? American guys are *so hot*. He just moved here last week. His dad's away on business, but I guess he's from here and they're moving back or something." Mikey's eyes shone. "He just punched Dewey Verbinski in the nose," he added gleefully. "I think he broke it!"

"He did *what*?"

"Dewey came up to us and called us faggots, basically," Mikey said. "Me and Adrian. So Adrian punched him in the face. He stuck up for me!"

Wroxy was silent for a moment, then she said, "Mikey, he probably just didn't like Dewey calling him a faggot. It probably had nothing to do with you. Don't go blowing this up into something it isn't."

Even as she said it, Wroxy felt vile. She wanted to be happy for Mikey, who seemed transported by bliss, but she realized that she was also tasting jealousy in her own right. On one hand, she had always prized her primacy in Mikey's life, had based a substantial amount of her own identity on that sense of importance, and was sensitive about protecting it. On the other hand, the news that a tall, handsome blond knight in shining black leather had strode onto the battlefield of Auburn High School and redeemed Mikey's honour with one knockout punch was an uncomfortable reminder than no boy—or indeed, anyone else—had ever done that for her.

"Do you think he looks Goth?" Mikey said tentatively, attempting to reestablish their connection. He'd never seen Wroxy act this way and he was vaguely hurt and baffled by her unwillingness to allow him this moment of joy. "I mean, with the leather jacket and all? Is that the way those guys look in the clubs on Queen Street?"

"Yeah, Mayberry Goth," Wroxy sneered. "Your buddy looks a little too wholesome to be full-on Goth." She couldn't bring herself to add how much Adrian's clean blondness—the opposite of the darkness she herself cultivated—combined with the sheer, sure masculinity, excited her. Adrian was clearly not a jock in the Shawn Curtis and Jim Fields mould. Everything about him— from the serene blue gaze, to the leather jacket and the chains on his wrist—exuded autonomy and fierce independence from convention. Whatever he was, he wasn't a team player. And in spite of what she had said to Mikey, she was stunned that this nineteen-year old boy, who could not only move, but triumph, in any milieu he chose, had defended Mikey physically, and in public.

Jesus, am I jealous of Mikey? Impossible! The essential Wroxy was appalled at this absurd notion. But the seditious, jilted-girl part of her, the one she hadn't realized she had, was far from sure. During the tenure of their friendship, neither of them had been courted by others. The notion of one of them falling in love, let alone the notion of anyone falling in love with *them*, wouldn't have occurred to either Wroxy or Mikey.

"Okay, so how about that talk?" Wroxy said. "How about you tell me what's been going on with you lately? We still have time before the bell rings. How about it?"

Mikey eyed her strangely. "You know what, Wrox? I think I'd like to be alone for a bit now. I don't feel like talking about bad stuff, or thinking about it. I'm going to try to focus on the future and think about positive things. I don't want to dwell on the past. It's been too ugly."

"Are you saying our friendship is in the past?"

"No, that's not what I'm saying at all. It's just that all you seem to want to do is talk to me like I'm 'poor Mikey' who can't seem to get his shit together, who cries all the time. You act like I'm pathetic."

"That's not fair and you know it," she said fiercely. "I've always been there for you."

"I know you have, and I've always been there for you, too. But look what happens when a guy comes along who puts some muscle between me and that asshole Dewey Verbinski. You act like there's something wrong with me for being happy about it. You act like the guy doesn't think I might be worth liking on my own or sticking up for. I would have thought you'd be happy for me that I have—"

"Have what?" Wroxy shocked herself as well as Mikey with the shrillness she heard in her own voice. "Are you about to say 'a boyfriend'? Because," she said, sounding shrewish, even to herself, "you don't. Look, I'm glad he stuck up for you this once, but don't count on it happening all the time. Look at how much trouble your stupid crushes have already gotten you into."

"A new friend," Mikey said quietly. "I was about to say I would have thought you'd be happy for me that I have a new friend, that's all."

He gathered up his books and walked in the direction of the maintenance shed, leaving his lunchroom tray behind, as Adrian had done. He didn't look back to where Wroxy was standing open-mouthed, wondering what had just happened between them.

Adrian was waiting for him after school. He was leaning up against the wall next to the front entrance, smoking a cigarette in plain sight. The fact that this was against the rules, and that Adrian didn't seem to care about rules, excited Mikey.

"Hey," Adrian drawled. "I thought I should maybe walk you home. Especially with what happened at lunchtime with Verbinski. Do you mind?"

Do I mind? Not in this lifetime. Aloud, Mikey said, "No, I don't mind. That'd be great. Thanks." He thrilled to the sound of Adrian's voice and was immediately suffused with warmth as he stepped into his protective shadow. Mikey felt very small and vulnerable, and for the first time didn't feel those things to be liabilities. He glanced down at Adrian's large, capable hands. They were neither bruised nor scratched in spite of that collision with Dewey Verbinski's face hours earlier. "It's funny to hear you call him that, 'Verbinski.' Just his last name, like he was a nobody."

"Why?" Adrian flicked the cigarette butt onto the ground. "He *is* a nobody."

"People either call him 'Dewey' or 'Dewey Verbinski.' It's almost as though he's their god or something, not someone you'd ever call by his last name. Like, it would be disrespectful."

Adrian laughed shortly. "He's a weenie." He took Mikey's books from his arms and leaned them against his own hip, carrying them as they walked. "I think the world would be better off without him and people like him, don't you?"

"More than anything," Mikey said fervently. "I wish he were dead, or gone. He's a terrible person."

"Who's that friend of his? The other one, with the black hair? After they sent Verbinski to the nurse's office, he and some other guys were looking at me and whispering." Adrian smiled. "I don't think they liked the fact that I hit their . . . what did you call him? Their 'god'? I think they're going to try to mess with me. Likely more than one on one, too."

"Oh God." Mikey gasped. "I didn't even think of that. I hope I don't get you into trouble."

"I can handle myself." Adrian shrugged. "Don't worry. Hey, speaking of getting into trouble, what's the deal with that girl, Wroxy? Your friend? Hope I didn't cause a problem there. I didn't mean to."

"She'll get over it. She's been a bit weird lately." Mikey felt like a traitor saying the words. "We've been best friends forever. Some stuff happened to me last month with those guys. They hurt me a little, and she's been worried. She's way overprotective."

"Those guys? The same ones?"

"Yeah."

"Why do they hate you so much?" Adrian looked straight ahead. The sun was beginning to yield to shadows, and his blond-stubbled profile was outlined in late-afternoon light. His jaw was clenched, giving him an impassive look, like the photographs Mikey had seen of the marble sarcophagi of fallen paladins in the cathedrals of Europe. Mikey yearned to press closer to Adrian, to feel the stiff leather jacket through his own nylon windbreaker.

"They call me things, you know? I dunno." Mikey felt suddenly ashamed of the words he would have to use. He couldn't bear to say them. "They say I'm . . . well, you know. Not like a normal guy. More like a girl, you know?"

Adrian reached over and put his arm around Mikey's shoulders, pulling him in close. Mikey felt a stirring below the waist as the beginning of a painful erection strained against the front of his jeans.

"That's not such a bad thing, Mikey," Adrian said. "Sometimes it's kind of nice to be with a different kind of guy. Girls aren't everything, trust me. Do you know what I mean?"

"Do you have a girlfriend?" Mikey asked. His voice cracked. "I mean, here or back in Connecticut?"

"No," Adrian said. "Not right now. Let's not talk about that, okay?" He reached up and caressed the outside of Mikey's neck. The touch of Adrian's fingers against the sensitive skin of Mikey's throat was like an electric current of nearly unbearable pleasure. He closed his eyes, only dimly aware that they were still walking and Adrian was guiding him. He had no doubt that Adrian wouldn't let him fall. He was also aware that he was being touched in public by another boy, in plain sight of anyone who happened to be looking out their front picture windows. For once, he didn't care. His entire world was reduced to those fingers on his neck and the throbbing heat that flowed upwards from his groin.

Adrian leaned down and whispered in his ear. "Are your parents home? Can we go up to your room?"

Mikey shook his head in answer to the first question, then nodded in answer to the second, completely incapable of verbalizing.

Adrian seemed to understand. He moved his hand down Mikey's back, resting just above his ass. He propelled him gently forward.

They turned onto Webster Avenue and walked halfway down the street to Mikey's house.

"This is where I live," Mikey said. The windows were dark. His parents weren't home from Windsor yet. Then Mikey remembered the telephone message from his mother telling him that they weren't due home till later tonight.

The hallway was very dark.

Adrian put his arms around Mikey's waist and pulled him in close. He turned his head to the side and gently lowered his lips to Mikey's, kissing him hard. Mikey felt the pressure of Adrian's teeth beneath his chapped lips, the unfamiliar scrape of Adrian's stubble against his soft cheek and the insistent pressure of Adrian's mouth on his. Mikey tasted cigarette smoke and spearmint. Adrian slid his hand down the back of Mikey's jeans. His index finger teased the uppermost part of the cleft of Mikey's ass, then his whole hand slipped in, cupping the cheek possessively.

"My room is upstairs," Mikey breathed. "Come up. It's this way."

"Leave the lights off," Mikey whispered. "Please?"

"No," Adrian said, switching on the bedside lamp. "I want you to see me. I want your eyes on my body." He shrugged off the leather jacket, letting it drop to the floor. Slowly, Adrian pulled the red t-shirt over his head, exposing the flat stomach and broad, compact chest. Tufts of gold hair nestled beneath Adrian's muscle-corded arms. A mat of the same dense, dark-blond hair bisected his pectoral muscles, trailing down in a column that vanished beneath the waistband of his jeans. The outline of Adrian's thick, trapped penis, slanting upward, was clearly visible against the faded denim. Adrian locked eyes with Mikey. Never breaking contact, he unhooked his belt and unbuttoned his jeans, sliding them down across his narrow hips. He kicked them off and stood there, unsmiling, naked and silent.

Mikey reverenced what he saw before him. Adrian's erection, free of the confines of his jeans speared away from his body. To Mikey it was the most beautiful thing he had ever seen. In the soft, warm light of the lamp, Adrian's skin glowed like phosphorus.

Mikey blushed at the perfection. He looked up into Adrian's face, searching for reassurance. Adrian's smile was tender as he opened his arms. Mikey noticed the tattoo just above the left triceps, but in the shadows of the bedroom he couldn't make it out.

"Take your clothes off and come here," Adrian said. "Come to me."

Mikey hesitated only a moment, then began to undress. When Mikey was naked, Adrian stepped forward and took him into his arms. Adrian lowered him gently onto the bed, spreading Mikey's legs with his own knees. Adrian balanced his weight on his knees, lowering his pelvis so that his erection brushed against Mikey's. Supine beneath Adrian's body, he gasped at the erotic shock of the contact. His arms extended and striated, palms flat on the bed. Adrian began to kiss Mikey's face and body. He traced his tongue down Mikey's chest, pausing to flick his nipples with the tip of it.

Mikey's body was alive with sensations he had never dreamed of, with pleasure both unimaginable and, he felt, nearly beyond endurance. Tentatively at first, and then with more boldness, his hands explored Adrian's broad, scalloped back. His fingers traced the outline of Adrian's ass, feeling the hard indentations of muscle beneath skin that was surprisingly soft. He probed farther with his fingers, exploring the thicker, longer hair lining the cleft between the cheeks of his ass. Mikey swam in abasing, submissive lust. He longed to show Adrian that there was nothing he wouldn't do for him. He guided Adrian's hips upward, toward his head. Then he took Adrian in his mouth, wondering at the taste of heat and salty wetness. Adrian groaned in pleasure, a deep, guttural sound that came from low in his throat. As Mikey sucked, he thrilled at the power he felt. Adrian thrust his hips harder and Mikey gagged, then relaxed, the rhythm of his own ministrations matching that of Adrian's thrusts.

Above him, Adrian gracefully rotated his body and lowered his own mouth to Mikey's cock.

The sensation was immediate. Mikey arched his back as Adrian expertly teased along the shaft, tonguing the head. Mikey closed his eyes and felt a boiling tension that seemed to come out of nowhere and everywhere. He felt his groin clench, then suddenly, he erupted in a shattering climax. His body jerked as though he were being electrocuted, and spasm after spasm wracked his frame. Adrian's mouth fastened on Mikey's cock, refusing to release it. Mikey thrashed against the sheets, his fingernails raking Adrian's back and ass as though Mikey were drowning and Adrian were the only one who could offer succor. Then slowly the thrashing subsided. Adrian released him, then rolled over on the bed, taking Mikey in his arms and holding him close to his chest as the spasms wracking his body dwindled, then ceased altogether. Adrian threw one leg possessively across both of Mikey's.

Gently, Adrian asked, "How was that? Are you okay?"

"Yeah," Mikey said. "I'm more than okay. I'm great. You?"

"I'm great, too," Adrian whispered into Mikey's ear. "Have you ever done that before? I mean, with a guy?"

"No, not with a guy. Not with anyone."

"So I'm your first?" Mikey sensed rather than saw Adrian's smile. "Cool." He hugged Mikey tightly. "What an honour."

"Hey," Mikey said. "What's that tattoo on your arm? I like it. It looks like a scarab or something, right? It's sexy."

Adrian propped himself up on one elbow and leaned into the aureole of the bedside lamp so Mikey could see his left triceps clearly.

"It tells a story, see?" Adrian said. "My story. It's a broken heart with an eye at the centre, with a tear coming out of it. Above it, there's an eternal flame." Mikey stared at the tattoo in wonder. Adrian leaned his arm close to Mikey's face so that Mikey could see it more clearly. "The sides of it have spikes, like legs. Five on each side, ten in total. It's a bastardized version of the sacred heart from Catholic mythology. I based it on having my heart broken in love so many times and having cried so much. The eternal flame is for the fire that will never go out inside me, no matter how much pain the heart can take. The spiky legs," he said, pointing, "are to keep others away from the vulnerable heart. Plus," he added, flexing his biceps, "it makes me look mean and tough."

"Wow. That's incredible. I've never heard anything so beautiful."

"I thought you might be able to relate," Adrian said. He caressed Mikey's hair. "I knew you'd understand. Let's just keep it a secret, though. Okay? I mean, all of this. Let's just have it be you and me. That way we can do this whenever we want to. I have other stuff to show you."

"Yes." His joy was all-encompassing. "We should keep it between us. We won't tell anyone," he said, thinking of Wroxy. "It'll be our secret."

"I love you, Mikey." Adrian kissed Mikey's chest and ran his tongue along Mikey's nipples. "I want you to love me, too. I want to be your boyfriend. You know you want one, and I want to be him."

Mikey, too transported with joy and unprecedented completion to even think beyond the immediacy of Adrian's words, merely sighed and nodded. Then Adrian's ascendant mouth was on his, and he felt himself stirring to life beneath the driving weight of Adrian's body.

Jim Fields heard the stones against his windowpane but, still half asleep, didn't identify the sound right away. He sat up in bed and rubbed his eyes. The scattershot of pebbles came again, and he swung his legs over the side of the bed, padded naked to the window and looked outside.

In the yard, standing in a circle of light from the back porch, was his best friend, Dewey Verbinski. He mimed opening a window, gesturing to Jim that he should open his own.

As always Jim obeyed, nearly by instinct.

"Hey," Dewey called out from the front yard. He sounded distraught. "Come on down. I want to talk to you."

Jim looked at the clock on his dresser. It was three A.M. He looked out the window. Dewey waved again. "Come on, Fields. Come down here. We have to talk."

"Shhhhh!" Jim whispered loudly. "You're gonna wake my fucking parents! It's three in the morning. Are you high? What's wrong with you?

"Jim, please." Dewey's voice was pleading. "It's an emergency. I've done something terrible, man. I'm really freaked out and I have to talk to you. Come on, man. Be a friend. Please? Come down. I'm begging you. I need your help."

"All right, hold on. But keep quiet. If my parents know you're out there, I'm going to be up shit creek. Just stay there, okay? Don't come near the house."

Jim dressed quickly from the jumble of clothes on the floor at the foot of his bed, a sweater and a pair of nylon track pants. He hurried down the stairs in to the kitchen. He unlocked the kitchen door and stepped out into the backyard. The cold was biting. Jim wished he'd grabbed a jacket.

"What is it, Dewey?" Jim whispered. "I'm serious. Are you on drugs? You're going to get me grounded again."

"Oh, man, I've really done it this time. I think I've killed an *actual person*."

Jim peered into Dewey's face. Tears glinted at the corners of Dewey's eyes, a surreal enough image to Jim, who had never seen Dewey shed a tear under any circumstances.

"Who?" Jim asked dumbly. "Who did you kill?"

"Oh, man." Dewey was moaning now. "The Childress faggot. I couldn't help myself. He came on to me. Can you believe it? After everything we did? I hit him *so* hard. I think he's dead. He's not moving."

"What the *fuck*?" Jim was now fully awake and dreadfully aware that this was no joke. Whatever had upset Dewey was real. For the first time he entertained the possibility that Dewey had actually snapped and gone over the edge. This was nothing like their baiting of the Childress faggot, and what Jim thought of as mere teasing. "What are you telling me, Dewey? Are you fucking serious?"

"You have to come. Please, Jimbo. You need to help me. I don't know what to do."

"Where did you leave him? You know, the body?"

"The field," Dewey said. He gestured toward the dark sprawl of mutilated farmland on the other side of the street upon which Jim's subdivision had been built. "Over there—see?"

Jim peered into the night. "I don't see anything."

"Come on, it's over there."

"You killed him next to my *house*? Are you *nuts*?"

"Come on!" Dewey dashed ahead into the darkness. "We need to hurry!"

Jim scrambled after him, trying to keep up. His feet, naked inside the boots he'd shoved on, chafed against the stiff leather. Dewey was moving with an agility that Jim had never seen, nimbly skipping across the frozen earth in a way that seemed incongruous given his bulk.

This better be serious, Jim thought irritably as he tried to follow Dewey's sprinting shape. *This had better not be some kind of pathetic practical joke.*

"Over here," Dewey called out. He'd stopped running and was standing twenty-five yards in front of Jim. The night was very black, and Jim could barely make out Dewey's shape. He turned to look at the subdivision behind him, which now seemed very far away. Then he jogged over to where Dewey was standing motionless.

"All right, where's Childress?" Jim demanded. He looked down at the ground but saw nothing,

Dewey covered his mouth with his right hand. He giggled. "He must have left," Dewey said. "I could have sworn he was right here."

"Fuck, Dewey, this is bullshit! You dragged me all the way out here at three in the morning for some stupid joke? I was sleeping, man!" Jim turned his back on Dewey and began to walk back toward his house.

"Jim?" Dewey called. "Jim, turn around. There's something I want to show you. Come here."

Jim turned around. "What?"

Dewey cocked an index finger, beckoning him over. "Just come here, Jim. Please? It'll only take a second. I'm sorry, dude. I need to explain why I brought you out here."

"I think that punch you took to the nose this afternoon rattled your brains," Jim grumbled.

Then he stopped, confused. Jim peered more closely at Dewey's face. Something was wrong. He shook his head, trying to rid it of the last vestiges of sleep. When he'd left Dewey after school, his nose had been swollen to the size of a tennis ball, and both of his eyes had been scored with black bruises from the new kid's punch.

But now Dewey's face was unblemished. His nose was unbroken, and there were no bruises beneath the glittering eyes. Jim took a few stumbling steps backward and whispered, "You're not Dewey."

Dewey took two steps toward Jim and placed both of his hands on Jim's shoulders. Jim felt impossibly strong fingers dig into the soft flesh of his upper arms. They pulled Jim close.

"No. I'm not," Dewey said in a cold, dry voice that sounded nothing like Dewey's.

Jim gasped as the thing in Dewey's shape lowered its mouth down on his and kissed him full and hard. Jim felt it sucking at his tongue, probing. He struggled against its viselike grip, but he was implacably held. He felt a blinding sheet of pain and an explosion of hot blood flooding his mouth. He choked as a torrent of hot, salty copper ran down his throat. Jim gagged and stumbled backward.

The thing in Dewey's shape spit Jim's severed tongue onto the dark earth. The lower half of its face was bathed in Jim's blood. It licked its gleaming red teeth and Jim realized it was smiling. Jim tried to scream, but nothing would come from his throat except an agonized, frog-like croak. He fell and hit his head against what felt to him like a sharp rock on the ground. Through eyes crazed with pain, Jim tried to focus as Dewey's body shimmered and rippled, running like wax, forming and reforming into shapes that were alternately human and bestial. For a moment Jim was staring at Mikey Childress. Then he had a vivid, oddly familiar impression of blond hair and blue eyes, and the flash of something dark and oily, like a leather jacket.

And suddenly it was Dewey again. Or rather, Dewey with skin gone leathery and dark, with fur-covered hands that had become claws ending in long yellow nails.

Then Dewey was gone altogether and nothing remained but a monster from beyond Jim's worst nightmares, a creature with shining red eyes and a maw full of meat-ripping teeth from which issued breath that was foul beyond measure. Jim tried to turn his face away from the stench, but the creature tangled its fingers in Jim's hair, brutally forcing his head in place, forcing him to see, to hear, to smell.

"I've wanted you since I first saw you," the creature said. It licked its lips in a horrible parody of lust. "Did you know I have a photo of you with your shirt off tacked up on the wall over my desk at home? I jack off to it all the time. Do you jack off thinking of me, too?"

Jim shook his head wildly from side to side and tried to scream again, nearly passing out from the agony that came knocking. He heard a sound like massive sails flapping in the wind as two enormous black wings unfurled, almost languorously, from the creature's back. Jim guessed that each membrane spanned twelve feet from shoulder to tip.

It reached down, almost lovingly, and picked Jim up in its arms, cradling him like a paramour. "I'm going to fuck you to death," it said. The creature slipped a long talon down the back of Jim's track pants, cutting a bloody strip along his tailbone. Jim made a mewling sound and whipped his head back and forth, once again close to blacking out from the pain. Its fingernail rent the nylon fabric of Jim's track pants as though it were made of wet tissue. It probed Jim's anus with the razor-sharp tip, finding purchase, teasing the outer ring of his sphincter. When it impaled him, penetrating the tender skin of the rectum, pushing in deeper, shredding the flesh to tatters with two quick sawing motions, Jim finally found the voice to shriek. "And then, I'm going to eat you alive. Or maybe I'll eat you alive first, *then* fuck you. We have all night to get to know each other, and we've waited a long, long time."

Suddenly Jim was airborne. The sound of flapping wings was like a thunderclap in his ears. Looking down, he saw the ground fall away. He caught a glimpse of his dwindling house far below. His last conscious thought before he passed out from pain and loss of blood was that his parents would never know what had happened to him.

Dimly he wished that he'd been a better son.

Then Jim yielded to blackness as the blanket of cold stars against the night sky was momentarily shadowed by enormous wings that flapped toward the escarpment.

In the field, night scavengers had already scented Jim's freshly spilled blood. By dawn they had eaten his tongue, leaving no trace of him for anyone to find.

Just before dawn, three disparate dreamers tossed fitfully in their sleep, each trapped by nightmares unique to them, or so they would have naturally assumed.

Dewey Verbinski, breathing with difficulty through his bandages, dreamed he was being pursued by a large bird. He heard wings flapping, but when he looked up, there was nothing hunting him. Still, he ran through an alien landscape. With the sludgy counter-logic of dreams, the harder he ran, the slower he moved. As the gigantic shadow fell across his path, he tried to look up but found himself unable to. He woke up gasping for air, looking wildly around his dark room, listening for the sound of wings.

Wroxy Miller dreamed that she and Mikey were fighting. The reason for their anger wasn't clear, but it seemed to be about—who? A boy? Adrian? Yes, there he was, with his arm around Mikey who looked at her with scalding pity. "Things are going to be different, Wroxy," he said sadly. "They couldn't have stayed this way. I don't need you. I have Adrian now. Friendships weren't made to last. Ours sure wasn't."

Wroxy woke to a damp pillow. Her eyes were sore, her hair sealed to her wet face. Because she was a pragmatist at heart, she consigned the dream to her subconscious, making a mental note to address this situation with Mikey tomorrow. Wroxy believed that dreams were omens and signs, and this one was a sign that trouble was coming.

For his part, Mikey had fallen asleep without showering after Adrian had left. He'd run his fingers along his awakened body and had traced the letter *A* across his sticky-dried belly.

His dreams were inchoate, but sweet enough to keep him asleep until well after sunrise.

Mikey and Wroxy tried to make reparations to the fissure in their friendship the next morning, but both were withdrawn and vaguely resentful. They walked in silence, each hoping the other would see his or her presence as enough of a gesture. At any other time Mikey would have called her the night before to tell her that he and Adrian had made love, but now he intended to wait until a moment opportune enough to guarantee a warm reception from her.

The first thing they noticed as they walked to school together the next morning was the two police cars parked outside the main doors of the high school.

"This is weird," Wroxy said. "I wonder what's going on?"

"Two police cars, not just one. Drugs, maybe?"

"In this school?" Wroxy sounded doubtful. "Maybe steroids for those meatheads on the hockey team, but they probably get them from their coach. Come on, let's go inside. Maybe someone in there knows."

"I hope Adrian's all right. I hope Dewey didn't pull anything with him later, after Adrian beat him up."

"Adrian didn't 'beat him up,' Mikey. Adrian broke his nose. *You* got beaten up. Dewey got punched. And I'm sure your precious Adrian can take care of himself."

"Are you saying that because you feel sorry for me or because you don't like Adrian? Fact is, no one has ever punched anyone in the face for messing with me before, so if I want to call it 'beating up,' that should be okay with you. Right?"

"Whatever, Mikey," Wroxy said. "He's not the only one who has ever stuck up for you. Just remember that."

"You sound jealous, Wrox. What's the matter? I have a guy who likes me, and you don't? That's a problem for you, huh?"

Wroxy, who would rather have died than let on how badly Mikey's words had hurt her, gave a short, curt laugh. "Oh, he 'likes' you?" she jeered. "Mikey, get a grip. He's not your boyfriend. He's not even gay. *You're* the gay one here, no one else. As soon as Adrian gets settled into this school, he'll be sniffing after Gwen Horlick like a dog in heat, just like every other guy here. You watch."

"Yeah, well, maybe he will," Mikey said viciously. "Gwen's pretty, and she's not fat. She wears colours other than black, and her makeup doesn't make her look like a slut. Guys like that in a girl, you know. Or maybe you don't know, since you don't have a boyfriend."

His words brought a sting of tears to her eyes. "Well, at least I'm a real girl," she said, hating the words and hating the way she sounded as she said them. "I *will* have a boyfriend someday because I'm normal. I'm not going to always be some wimpy closet-case fag who cries all the time."

"You cunt," Mikey said helplessly. "Fuck you, Wroxy. Have a nice life."

Mikey turned his back on Wroxy and sat down. He was trembling with hurt and rage. Glancing back, he saw Wroxy walk to the back of the homeroom class with her head down. She looked like she might be crying, but he didn't care. He spotted Adrian waiting for him next to his seat. Adrian brightened visibly when he saw Mikey and waved him over, smiling.

"Hey, I missed you this morning," Adrian said as Mikey sat down. "Where were you? I was hoping we could walk to school together."

"Sorry, I had to talk to Wroxy. Probably the last time, too."

"What happened? Nothing serious, I hope?"

Mikey shrugged. "Who needs a best friend?" he said bitterly. "Not me, that's for sure."

Adrian reached his hand underneath Mikey's desk and squeezed his thigh. "You have one. You have me, remember?"

"Yeah, well . . . that's different. You're like . . . well, you said you love me. I love you, too," Mikey said, feeling light-headed to be saying the words aloud. "She's—she was—different. More like a sister."

"You don't need a sister." He squeezed Mikey's thigh harder. "Or a best friend. I want to be everything to you."

"You already are," Mikey murmured, meaning it.

34

By lunchtime the news of Jim Fields' disappearance had traversed the school. Most noted that if it had been Dewey, there might be less cause for alarm, but Jim was, for the most part, a straight arrow. His parents were frantic. Over the course of the morning the police had called several of Jim's friends to the office and asked them questions. No one knew anything. Yes, Jim seemed happy. No, he had never talked about running away. Yes, it did seem weird. No, he didn't have a girlfriend that anyone knew of, though he hadn't been short on offers or interest.

Wroxy found Mikey and Adrian sprawled on the lawn at the edge of the school property eating lunch. From a distance, Wroxy had to admit that she barely recognized him. Worse, that he looked good. In Adrian's company, the furtive, frightened sissy was transformed into someone she hardly knew. All of which made this overture even more bitter than she could have imagined.

"Hey," Wroxy said levelly. "I want to talk to you."

They stopped laughing. Adrian silently examined the tie of his boot. Mikey looked at Wroxy, noting that she looked like shit. That didn't please Mikey as much as he thought it might have, but he still stared at her coldly.

"What do you want? This had better be an apology."

"You're in no position to demand apologies, Mikey. Besides, if it was an apology, I'd make it in private. This isn't private."

"Whatever you want to say in front of me, you can say in front of Adrian."

"I'll take that under advisement, dude. As I said, this isn't an apology. In the meantime, have you heard about Jim?"

"Jim?" His tone was mocking. "Jim who?"

"Jim Fields. Remember? The previous love of your life?"

"What about him?" Mikey fanned his fingers and examined his nails, an affectation he'd stolen from Gwen Horlick because he thought it looked cool when she did it, though he would have died rather than admit its provenance.

"He disappeared," Wroxy said flatly. "He's gone."

Mikey shrugged. "So? What do you want me to do about it?"

"Aren't you curious?"

"Roxanne," Mikey said, deliberately using the name she hated. "The guy made my life a living hell. I don't care where he's gone. I just hope he stays there. Better still, I hope he comes back and takes Dewey Verbinski with him."

Adrian laughed softly at Mikey's words.

"Something funny, Adrian?" Wroxy's voice was cold. "Not that this has anything to do with you."

"Actually, Wroxy, it does. Everything and *everyone*," Adrian said, lingering over the word, "who bothers Mikey is my business now."

"Oh yeah? Who died and made you his protector? You just arrived here and suddenly you're Mikey's white knight?"

"Well, someone had to be," Adrian said mildly. "You weren't doing a very good job."

Wroxy stared at Adrian, then looked to Mikey. "Are you going to let him talk to me like that? Is that okay with you?"

"What did you call me?" Mikey drawled. "I think your exact words were 'a wimpy closet-case fag who cries all the time.'"

Adrian scowled. "She called you that?"

"You called me a cunt," Wroxy shot back. "We're even."

"You *are* a cunt," Mikey said dismissively. "And I'm not crying anymore. So we're *not* even. Now, get lost, cunt." He made a shooing gesture with his hands.

"I wouldn't stay if you paid me, faggot," Wroxy said. "You know what? They were all right about you here. This town has your number, big time."

"*Had*," he corrected her. "Not *has*. I'm not the same anymore."

"No, you're worse." Wroxy pulled her sunglasses out of her knapsack and put them on before she walked away. She didn't look back this time.

"Good riddance," Mikey said tightly. He forced the tears back before they came.

"Shall we kill her?" Adrian's blue eyes were guileless.

Taken aback, Mikey said, "No, of course not. Wait, you're kidding, right?" He laughed uncertainly. "Of course you're kidding. Stupid me. Just ignore me."

"I could never ignore you." Adrian leaned over and kissed Mikey on the mouth before Mikey could ask him if he was crazy to kiss him in public.

As October burned in the trees, and the sky that framed Auburn hung like a stained-glass window of red, yellow, and blue, Adrian and Mikey grew inseparable.

In the mornings, Adrian would wait for Mikey at the end of Webster Avenue and walk him to school. In Adrian's company, Mikey felt completely safe, and he began to change. He stood taller and straighter. He became more concerned with his clothes and personal grooming, not wanting to be anything but his best for Adrian. He wished he was beautiful, or handsome, but he satisfied himself that even if he wasn't, Adrian still wanted him.

His mother was the first to notice the subtle transformation and was puzzled by it.

"You look nice today, honey," she said at breakfast. She'd looked up, confused, as though something was out of place in her well-ordered kitchen. "You look different."

It wasn't until Mikey left the house that Donna realized that her son had looked her directly in the eyes, and the miasma of fear and furtiveness that always trailed after Mikey like a cape was nowhere to be seen.

After school, during the two-and-a-half-hour safety zone

between the end of classes and his parents' return from work, Mikey and Adrian made love on his narrow bed.

Adrian seemed to genuinely glory in all of Mikey's oppositeness from him. Adrian bent his superb body to Mikey's pleasure, kissing and touching him in places he had never dreamed of being kissed or touched. He cradled Mikey's smaller, frailer body against his powerful one but also used him with an authority that left Mikey faint with lust, feeling not only physically desired but devoured.

He loved to watch Adrian's nude body as he walked around Mikey's bedroom—the way the narrow waist tapered; the muscular legs, the broad back and shoulders, the cabled arms, the tattoo, as though nakedness was his natural state and clothes merely an afterthought.

The first time Adrian fucked him, slick with spit and hand lotion, he held Mikey close during the initial pain, then for a long while afterward. The idea of feeling so physically complete, so *right*, had never even occurred to Mikey except in his fantasies during what felt like the endless, spiralling eons before Adrian's arrival. A small stream of Mikey's tears—for once, tears of joy and surrender—pooled in the hollow of Adrian's shoulder as Mikey lay against him, caressing the find blond hair of Adrian's dense forearms.

"My mom wants to meet you," Mikey said one evening in the second week of October. They were sitting on a bench in Rotary Park watching the autumn leaves in descent. "I've mentioned you a couple of times. She's curious about you."

Adrian said, "I don't really 'do' parents," he said. "Parents creep me out. I can barely deal with my own father, you know what I mean?" He took a drag of his cigarette and blew smoke in the air, something Mikey thought made him look tough and incredibly sexy.

"You look like James Dean when you do that," Mikey told him.

Another time, Mikey asked him where he lived and why they never went to Adrian's house to make love after school. "We could stay longer, you know? Since your dad isn't there, we'd have the whole house to ourselves. I could tell my mother than I'm over at your house, studying."

"The house isn't finished yet, and it's really dirty," Adrian said. "I hate being there. I like your room. I like being around your stuff. You know what I mean?"

Mikey swooned, so deeply in love that he accepted Adrian's explanation with no other thought than that it might be nice to buy some vanilla-scented candles at the drugstore to make his room smell even more inviting to Adrian. In the school library he'd read in *Glamour* magazine that men loved the scent of vanilla. Mikey had tucked away this information and more, in case it might be something he could bring to Adrian in tribute to their love.

If he was sure of anything, it was this: he had found true love. This, he realized, must be what being *normal* felt like.

For her part, Wroxy watched Mikey and Adrian with a mixture of envy and growing mistrust. Mikey hadn't spoken to her since their fight. Since Adrian was always with him, getting him alone seemed impossible.

Because she missed him terribly, Wroxy had read her Tarot cards over the situation, asking the cards to tell her if she and Mikey would resolve their dispute. She was comforted by the answer: yes, they would resolve it. On the other hand, when she read her cards over Adrian, the results were puzzling.

She stared at the beautifully wrought, gilt-edged Death card in her hand, the image of a black-robed child standing in a field under a rising sun, holding a white rose in its hand. The Death card signified transition, passage, and transformation.

Wroxy reasoned that she was being shown Adrian's effect on Mikey, and his life. To be sure, something about Adrian seemed to intimidate all the people who had previously hunted Mikey like small game. The boys left him alone. And to Wroxy's disgust and contempt, a few of the girls, notably Gwen Horlick, had begun speaking of Mikey as though his femininity was something "fabulous" and "wild," as though he were something from a television show instead of the same faggoty kid they'd all tormented for nearly a decade.

Wroxy had no doubt in her mind that Horlick's ultimate aim was Adrian's seduction—something Wroxy would have welcomed like a lottery win if she'd thought it would bring Mikey back to her.

Of the hardcore Mikey-haters, Dewey Verbinski seemed most committed to giving Mikey a wide berth. In the weeks since Jim's disappearance—which, after a flurry of interest from the police, was almost universally being spoken of as "a runaway situation," since there was no sign of any home invasion or forcible removal of Jim from his parents' house—Dewey had grown furtive and skittish without Jim by his side. He'd tried to tell the police about the dreams he'd had on the night Jim had vanished, dreams he'd been having nightly since then, but they only looked at him strangely and said they weren't investigating dreams. The police had heard rumours that the Verbinski boy was a bully, so his broken nose barely registered with them.

Stash and Yalda told Dewey that they felt sad about Jim being gone—*his poor parents!*—but that if he knew something about it that he wasn't telling, that was very bad.

The swelling around Dewey's broken nose had gone down, though the bruising remained. He assiduously avoided Adrian and Mikey. His new furtiveness was becoming conspicuous enough to elicit whispers of bewilderment from the other boys, bewilderment that soon blossomed into contempt. While this was a new and shameful state for Dewey, he bore it silently, with downcast eyes.

"I almost feel sorry for him," Mikey said to Adrian as they watched Dewey hurry out of the locker room after gym class. Adrian, as it turned out, could play basketball better than anyone else, including Shawn Curtis. "He seems lost without Jim."

"Remember what he did to you," Adrian replied. "He doesn't deserve your pity. Neither does Jim Fields."

"Still, it's sad to see."

Adrian shrugged. "Embrace hate."

Mikey stood stock-still. "What did you say?"

"What did I *say*? What do you think I said?"

"You said 'embrace hate.' I heard you. Why did you say that?"

"I didn't," Adrian said. "I said 'that's the way it goes.'"

"You did? Are you sure? That's not what I heard."

"Well, that's what I *said*. Why? What does 'embrace hate' mean?"

"Just something I saw on a website once." Mikey's throat felt very dry. "Don't worry about it."

"I won't. I'll meet you out by the back of the maintenance shed after school, okay? Then we'll go back to your place and hang out. I'm feeling really good today."

"All right," Mikey said faintly. He suddenly felt a terrible need to speak to Wroxy. "Wait, no, Adrian. I'm sorry. I can't this afternoon. I have to go to a doctor's appointment after school. My mom set it up a month ago."

"I'll walk you there," Adrian said. "Then home later."

"No," Mikey insisted. "It would look weird. I'd better go alone. I'm sorry Adrian. I'll see you tomorrow."

"You don't want to see me today? Are you serious?"

"I can't. I said I have a doctor's appointment."

"You're lying. You're going to see someone else."

"I'm not lying. I'll see you tomorrow."

"You're lying," Adrian said again. "It's because of what I said about Dewey Verbinski, isn't it?" Mikey heard thwarted fury beneath Adrian's words. "You said you hated him, remember? Why are you feeling sorry for him? Were you lying to me then, too?"

"I do hate him," Mikey said. "I've never lied to you, I promise. I have to go now, okay? Please, Adrian. I'll see you tomorrow, I promise."

"Do you love him like you loved Jim Fields?"

"What? I never told you I loved Jim Fields. I *don't* love Jim Fields. I love *you.*"

"You did love him. I could tell by how you talked about him, even with what he did to you. Aren't I enough for you?"

"I hate them both! I always have! You're more than enough for me."

"Remember that, then," Adrian said. "Never forget that."

Mikey gathered his things and hurried outside, leaving Adrian in the locker room. For his part, Mikey was more than confused. He had felt a glimmer of genuine fear for the first time in Adrian's presence.

Did he really say what I think he said? Mikey felt the blood thundering in his temples. *Could I have misheard him?*

Of course not. The second voice was more rational. *You heard him say the same words you found on that website. The ones you used for that spell. The one you never told anyone about, not even Wroxy. And he sounded . . . sly when he said it.*

"No he didn't," Mikey said aloud, defiantly. "He didn't say 'embrace hate.' He said 'that's the way it goes.' And that *is* the way it goes. He would never hurt me. He would never hurt anyone." Mikey regretted his lie about the doctor's appointment. Adrian deserved better.

You think those words sound alike? You think you could mistake them?

"Shut up," Mikey whispered. "Just shut up."

He hurried back into the school. When he reached the locker room, he looked around expectantly. "Adrian! Where are you? I forgot, the appointment isn't until next week!"

His voice echoed against the damp tiles, through the faint drifts of residual steam from the showers, but there was no answer in the empty room.

36

"You made your bed, Mikey, you lie in it," Wroxy said. "You've got some nerve coming to me at this point. I don't know if we're even still friends." She sat in a stiff-backed chair in front of her desk in the basement bedroom. Mikey had rarely seen her without makeup, and he was struck by how young she looked. "This guy comes out of nowhere and you dump me for him. You . . . *change*. That's the best way I can describe it. Now you want to tell me—just *now*, mind you—that you think there's something weird about the fact that he wants to be with you all the time?"

"I didn't say it was weird. It's not weird, it's nice—sort of. But he said something today that kind of freaked me out."

"What did he say?"

"I can't tell you."

"Why not?"

"It wouldn't make any sense." Mikey knew he was dissembling but he was still not prepared to tell Wroxy about killing the cat. And he couldn't tell her about the website or the spell without giving her all the details. "Couldn't you trust me, just this once?"

"I did trust you. That's the problem. We've been best friends for three years. I never once betrayed you. I kept all of your secrets. You turned on me and called me a cunt, remember?"

"I'm sorry." He was pleading. "Really, please forgive me."

"Have you had sex with this guy?" Mikey hesitated, then nodded. Wroxy's eyes widened. "Really? You've had, like, actual *sex* with him? He's *gay*?"

"I don't know if he's gay. He doesn't say he's gay. He just says he loves *me*."

"You don't know much, do you?" Wroxy was softening, her maternal instincts taking over in place of her anger. "Okay, what do you want me to do?"

"Could you read your cards? I need to know some things. I promise things will be different. I want our friendship back, for sure. And I want this thing to work out with Adrian as well. I love him. And I love you. Differently, of course, but the same. Well," he added, "you more."

"I did a reading on him once," Wroxy said, ignoring Mikey's words about their friendship with difficulty. "It all looked okay. It looked like you and I were going to be friends again, and it looked like he was helping you change—which you have."

"Please, read them again," he urged her, thinking of the undertone he'd heard in Adrian's voice in the locker room. "For me? Please?"

"All right. I'll get the cards." She lit some votive candles and spread her deck out on the floor in front of them. "We'll do a drawing of three. Pick three cards."

Mikey drew the first and held it up to Wroxy.

"The Queen of Swords? How weird."

"What does the Queen of Swords mean?" He looked at the card, which showed a dark-haired woman weeping.

"Well, it would appear to be you," Wroxy said. She sounded confused. "She often represents being blessed, or cursed, with insight or perception. This could refer to your coming out, or maybe to some new information you've received recently. Ring any bells?"

Mikey shook his head and said nothing. "It can also mean a person—usually a woman, mind you—but in your case the cards could be saying something about you being gay—in a phase of life where she temporarily becomes a sword. Sometimes it's a death card, but not usually. Are you okay?" Mikey nodded, still not speaking. Wroxy hesitated, then gestured toward the deck. "All right, pick the next card. This will be the one that shows the major influence on your life right now."

Mikey took a deep breath and drew the second card. He handed it to Wroxy without looking at it.

"Mikey, this can't be right." Wroxy went pale. "You drew the Devil." She pointed to the engraving of a goat-headed Satan, its right hand extended, fingers uplifted. "This card signifies great malice. It doesn't necessarily mean the literal Devil, but it's a seriously nasty card. What's going on?"

"I don't know," he whispered. "I don't know what's going on."

"Are you sure you want to draw the third card? That'll be the one that reveals the outcome of whatever it is you're going through. Maybe we should talk about what's happening with you before we go this route."

"No," he said fretfully. "I want to know." Mikey reached down and drew the third card. This time he turned it over and looked at it himself. The engraving was of a full red moon hanging suspended over a range of dark purple mountain peaks. He showed it to Wroxy. "What does this mean?"

"The moon card represents a yearning for fulfillment or enlightenment. It's been said to represent working through 'the dark night of the soul' as a way of reaching something better in the morning. It's not a bad card to draw, all told. Also, interesting since there's a lunar eclipse two nights from now, on Halloween. Remember? You and I were planning to get out and watch it."

"Does it mean anything else?"

It wasn't lost on Wroxy that Mikey had ignored the fact that she'd just reminded him that they'd planned to watch the Halloween lunar eclipse together.

"Well, Mikey, it also means false friends, betrayal and deception." She looked at him accusingly. "Were you asking any questions about you and me when you pulled that card? Were you thinking of us and our fight?"

"No," he said, thinking of Adrian. "I wasn't. My mind was clear, just like you taught me to keep it when we read. What do you think it all means?"

"I think it means you've got to watch yourself, I think it means, in a nutshell, that you've come by some information that you aren't sharing with me, and that there's something nasty at work in your life that you've let guide you. And I think it means that you're going to get your answers very soon, whether you want them or not."

"Am I going to be all right?"

"I hope so, dude." Wroxy took his hand in hers. "And I don't want to put down your precious Adrian, but as far as I can tell, he's the only new thing in your life, so just watch yourself. Okay?" She reached out and brushed a shock of hair off his forehead, something she'd done a hundred times before. "Are you sure you don't want to tell me what's going on?"

"I can't," he said, thinking of the way the rain had sluiced through the dead cat's dashed brains in the light of the sputtering fire that night in the forest. "Not now. Soon, I promise. Just not yet."

"Mikey, I have to ask." Wroxy faltered, then spoke again. "Did you do something to Jim?"

"No, I didn't."

"Did Adrian?

He opened his mouth to speak, then pressed his lips together. Then he said, "No, he didn't. Adrian would never hurt anyone."

The two officers believed they were responding to a routine domestic disturbance report on Dagenais Street when they pulled the squad car into the driveway of the prim split-level. The younger of the two, Jimmy Moretti, was the detachment rookie. He hated the idea of violence against women and the thought of locking up a wife beater got his testosterone flowing. His partner, Aaron Prothro, was the more seasoned of the two, and therefore less likely to bust in like a pent-up superhero.

Inside, the two cops couldn't make any sense of what the terrified, hysterical woman—who was neither bruised nor cut, ruling her out as the victim, much to Moretti's mixed relief and disappointment—was trying to tell them. The more they urged her to calm herself, the more hysterical she became, crossing herself repeatedly. The torrent of mingled English and Polish alternated with more of the screams that had alerted the neighbours in the first place.

From what they had been able to gather, the lady, Mrs. Verbinski, had been watching television in the living room. She'd heard a terrible crash, and then she'd heard her son begin to scream. She'd run upstairs as fast as she could. The room had been dark, she'd said, except for the lamp that had been knocked to the floor. By its light, she'd seen something—apparently her son, Karol, struggling with someone. Her exact meaning had been unclear, but in the middle of the keening and weeping they'd caught the word "wings," though it had come out as "vinks."

Eventually the two officers had to call for an EMS detachment. A sedated Mrs. Verbinski was taken to Milton District Hospital for observation. They hadn't yet been able to contact her husband, Stanislaus, who was making an out-of-town pickup for his manager at the warehouse where he worked.

As they waited for backup, the two officers stood in what they gathered was the boy's bedroom surrounded by broken glass, and twisted metal that looked as though it had once been a window frame. The power had gone out and the only light in the room came from their flashlights and the moonlight through the window.

Moretti said, "Before she went out, she said she didn't see who he was fighting with."

"You speak Polish?" Prothro snorted. "Who knew you'd actually serve some purpose?"

"She said that part in English. But yeah, I speak some Polish. My mother's family is Polish."

"Did she say anything you could understand?"

"Sounded to me like she was calling out to her kid, or calling to someone to bring him back to her. I heard *Karolka*—Karol, the kid's real name, and *blagam*, which I think means 'please.' *Jezusa* means 'Jesus,' obviously."

"She thought that Jesus took her kid?"

"No. She was calling out in Jesus' name."

"I remember this kid from the Fields investigation," Prothro said. "He's a big kid, tough. Rumoured to be a nasty piece of work. I don't see him losing a fight to anyone."

"What about all this glass? Maybe he jumped out the window to get away?" He looked out the window and frowned. "He'd break a leg. It's too high up."

"Not only that. Look at where the glass is."

Moretti looked down at his feet. "All over the floor. So?"

"Exactly. *On the floor*. So whoever broke the glass came *through* the window, not out of it."

Moretti laughed nervously. "So what are you saying? Something came flying through the window and carried the kid off? You mean, like a vampire or something? Two nights before Halloween? Weird fucking town." He started to hum the *Twilight Zone* theme song but stopped when he saw the expression on his partner's face. "Aaron?"

"Go look outside and see if there's any glass on the ground outside."

"Come on," Moretti said. "You're kidding, right?"

"Just go and look, rookie," Prothro snapped. "Make yourself useful, and don't touch anything."

"Oh *Christ*," Moretti said, bending down and picking something off the floor near the bed. "Hand me a tissue, would you? Oh fuck, I think I'm going to be sick."

"What is it?" Prothro looked down at the floor, trying to see.

Mutely his partner held up two severed fingers, still attached to part of a hand joint. The blood was still wet. They didn't look neatly severed or even torn. They looked as though an animal had bitten them off. Prothro shone his flashlight on the bloodstained carpet. The fibers gleamed wetly in his light.

"Why didn't we notice this before?"

"Too dark in here," Moretti said. "No light."

With the flashlight, Prothro followed the trail of blood across the floor to the window, where it stopped. He walked over to the window and played the light across the empty yard, looking for glass but finding none. In the sky above, the moon was nearly full.

"Jesus," Prothro said.

"What?"

"Get those fingers in the refrigerator!" Prothro barked. "If we find the kid, they can still attach them, but only if they're put on ice right away! Where the *fuck* is the backup I called for?"

Moretti began taking the stairs by twos. He stopped, then turned back. "She said something else," he said haltingly.

"What did she say?"

"She said *Diabel zabrat moje dzisciatko.*"

"What the hell does that mean?" Prothro barely glanced at his partner. This was going to be some shitstorm.

Moretti's face was ashen in the reflected moonlight from the open window. "It means, 'the Devil took my baby.'"

Mikey, wake up. Wake up. Mikeeeee.

He opened his eyes. The bedroom was dark, but he felt someone sitting astride him. The shape—clearly male—blocked the moonlight that came through the window. Mikey reached up and touched its arms. He smiled in the darkness, feeling warm, familiar flesh and sinew.

"Adrian," he whispered. "Am I still dreaming?"

"No, Mikey, you're awake. Can you feel my body?"

"Yes." He sighed. "What are you doing here? How did you get into the house? My parents—"

"Shhhhh. Your parents don't know I'm here. It doesn't matter how I got here. I'm here for you now. Turn the light on. I want to show you something."

Mikey reached over and switched on the light. The window was wide open. The curtains blew in the night breeze. The room was freezing.

Adrian was naked, covered with dirt and what Mikey first took to be dark smears of mud that crisscrossed his body like a child's finger-paint. Streaks of the same mud daubed the lower half of his face. He sat upright and leaned back against the headboard. The streaks were red, not brown.

Mikey drew a sharp intake of breath. "Jesus Christ, Adrian! What happened to you? Were you in an accident?"

"Oh, no. I'm fine. But I brought you a present. Here—close your eyes and open your hands."

Mutely, Mikey obeyed. He felt something he didn't recognize being placed in his palm, something cold and soft, like a smooth, cylindrical sponge or a sausage.

"Open your eyes," Adrian said. Mikey heard suppressed mirth in his voice. He opened his eyes and looked into his palm. It was an uncircumcised penis, the puckered foreskin grey and bloodless. The penis was tattered at the root.

Mikey recognized it immediately. He'd seen it in the shower room enough times. And he'd never forgotten the humiliation the time its owner had waved it in his face and asked him if he wanted to suck it.

"Jesus Christ." Mikey doubled over. A wave of hot vomit sprayed from his mouth, soaking the sheets and splattering Adrian's naked hips. The stench of it hit him almost immediately, and he disgorged a second time. Adrian didn't move.

"You said you hated him. So I hated him, too. Now he's gone. He'll never bother us again."

"You killed him? Adrian, oh my God. You killed *Dewey*?"

"I love you."

His eyes are red, Mikey thought dully. *Not blue. Why did I think they were blue? How could I have missed something as basic as the colour of his eyes?*

"I've always loved you, and I always will. I'll always protect you. You wanted revenge, remember? You asked for a hammer. You received a hammer. We hated them, and now they're gone." Adrian's visage began to blacken and decompose, the handsome features appearing to liquefy like wax.

This time when Mikey inhaled, the sound was like a whistling teakettle squeal of pure terror. "How do you know about that?"

The red eyes became incandescent. They blazed in the runny tallow that was now Adrian's face. Mikey still saw love there: horrible, unending, unforgiving love.

"I know *everything*," Adrian said.

At dawn on Halloween morning Mikey was waiting outside Wroxy's house. He'd risked calling and waking her mother, but Wroxy had answered the phone herself.

In her basement later, Mikey told Wroxy everything.

This time the hysteria he felt served to focus his thoughts rather than scatter them. Wroxy sat open-mouthed as Mikey told her about the gay bashing in September, about finding the revenge spell on the computer, about the night in the forest when he sacrificed the cat, about Adrian's appearance the next morning, and the aftermath.

As he spoke, Mikey's eyes shone wide and dark in his face. Sweat matted the sides of his temples and Wroxy briefly considered that maybe he had taken something, a thought she discounted just as quickly.

"I'm telling you the truth, I swear. I promise. You probably don't believe me, but I am."

"I have something to tell you, too," Wroxy said. "I went there, to that place on the escarpment. The place where you saw the witches and the sacrifice. Something happened to me there."

"What?" Mikey's voice was fearful. "What happened?"

"Magic," she said. "Nothing like what happened to you, but I know you're telling the truth."

"What have I done? How is any of this possible?"

Wroxy sighed. "I don't want to go all Van Helsing on you, but it looks like you raised a demon. You spilled blood. You asked for revenge. That's the sort of magic we witches don't do. It's bad stuff—you've fucked with something very, very dark."

"What am I going to do? Adrian—it—told me it was going to keep killing."

Wroxy spoke slowly. "Who else did you ask for revenge against? A spell has to run its course. Adrian might have been created just to kill the people you asked for revenge against. Or, if you asked for something more general, he might be around for a long time."

"I don't remember," Mikey said, beginning to weep. "I haven't slept. I'm so tired. I'm so afraid."

"Mikey, listen to me. You have to focus. Tonight is Halloween. The veil between the worlds is at its most permeable tonight. Those . . . *demon worshippers* or whatever they are will be celebrating a Sabbat tonight, if that's even what they call the holy nights. We need to go to them. Plus, it's the lunar eclipse. Tonight the earth and the moon will be perfectly aligned. The moon will pass nearly dead centre through the earth's shadow. It's a night of power. Maybe they can be reasoned with, and they'll help us send this thing back."

"And if not?"

"Then we're on our own, Mikey." Wroxy knelt down and gathered him in her arms. "We've always been on our own, haven't we? Just you and me, babe."

"He used to call me that," Mikey said softly. "He used to call me 'babe.'"

Wroxy was momentarily confused. "Who?"

"Adrian."

Police cars had been parked outside Auburn High School all day. In anticipation of a full-scale panic, the police were doing their best to keep the news of Dewey Verbinski's disappearance as low-key as possible until they had their bearings, but news like that was hard to keep quiet in a small town.

Mikey had sat in the principal's office as the police grilled him about his friendship with Adrian Johnson.

Where had they met? At school.

How were they connected? They had become friends on Adrian's first day of school.

Was there anything more? No.

Did Adrian ever hurt him? No, why would he?

He broke Dewey Verbinski's nose. Was there bad blood? No, just two guys settling a score—Dewey called Adrian a faggot and Adrian punched him in the nose. Nothing more.

Was Adrian homosexual? No.

Was Mikey homosexual?

"I think I want my parents, or a lawyer," Mikey said. "I don't want to answer any more of these questions, please."

"Mikey," Constable Prothro said, leaning toward Mikey with what he hoped looked like paternal compassion. "Where does your friend Adrian live? You know, we checked the school records, and there's no documentation about a transfer student named Adrian Johnson from Connecticut to Milton, Auburn, or Campbellville. Everyone says they saw it, but no one can find it now. Do you know anything about that?"

"He said his father was from here," Mikey said. "He said his father was coming back and that they'd be together."

"There's no record of a father, either. Your buddy seems to be a blank slate, even though, as I said, everyone claims to have seen his paperwork. Again, any thoughts?"

"I want to see my parents or a lawyer. I don't know anything about any of this."

"Stick close to home for the next day or so, would you, Mikey? Let's see what we can figure out about what's going on here."

Mikey had promised that he would.

In October, in Auburn, the Halloween streets are tinged with fire. From darkened porches jack-o-lanterns glare with slashed eyes lit by candles, and dead leaves blow through the deserted streets, tossed in the black night wind. The town is dappled in hues of orange and black. This year, the few children who were dared—or were allowed—to trick-or-treat were accompanied by parents who stayed close, wary that whatever force had come to spirit away the two young men should decide to come calling again.

In the night skies above Auburn, the full moon had turned the colour of blood.

The eclipse had begun at eight o'clock, and by nine-fifteen the moon began to cross from the penumbra, the lightest part of the planet's shadow, into the darkest heart of its umbra. By ten-thirty, when Mikey pulled up to Wroxy's house in his mother's car, the sky was filled with copper light as the moon moved into the earth's shade.

"Do you remember where we're going?" Wroxy asked him, climbing into the passenger seat. "Can you find your way back there?"

"What do you think?" Mikey said coolly. "Of course I can find it. So could you." To Wroxy something was different about him.

Mikey looked older tonight. The shape of the man he would eventually become was pressing against the flesh and bone of the boy he still was. His eyes looked very black by the light of the dashboard. "Do you doubt it?" He looked up at the moon burning like a hulking live coal in the black sky. "Do you doubt it at all, especially tonight?"

"No." Wroxy shivered at the sound of his voice. "Not tonight."

Mikey turned the key in the ignition and backed the car onto Wroxy's street. She stole a furtive glance at Mikey out of the corner of her eye as he drove. In the light of the dashboard his face seemed carved from shadow. She touched the front of her sweater where, beneath it, the silver pentacle lay against her breast.

Mikey stared straight ahead, saying nothing. He abruptly turned left off the main road. Wroxy peered out the window but saw nothing. After fifteen minutes of driving, she sensed the road widen and clear.

"Look there," Mikey said, pointing. "The fire. You see it? We're here."

Wroxy looked to the left, then to the right. Fifty yards away, she saw the bonfire. Mikey steered the car toward the light, then put it into park. He turned off the ignition and opened the door.

"Come on," he said. "We have to talk to these people. We need their help."

"I'm afraid," Wroxy said, pulling back. "This is a bad place." She reached for Mikey's arm, but he brushed it off.

"Come on. Let's get this over with. If we're going to send him back, we need their help. These are the only people who can help us."

The twelve robed figures stood motionless and silent in a semicircle around the outer edge of the fire. Sparks sputtered up into the night and the air was full of the scent of woodsmoke. The tallest of them, the man in the crimson robe decorated with gold symbols, stepped forward, arms open in a gesture of benediction.

"Hello, Mikey Childress." The man removed his half-hood. He looked vaguely familiar, though Mikey couldn't immediately place his face. The man's voice, however, was quite familiar. It was the goat-killing voice from his nightmares; the voice he'd imagined that night in August when he lay awake praying the phone wouldn't ring. "We've been expecting you."

"You know my name," Mikey said stupidly. "How do you know my name?"

"Do you really need to ask? My name is Kelvin Cowell. I'm your mother's pastor. But that isn't the only place I know you from. You *have* seen us before, haven't you? Only, the last time you visited us you didn't stay to introduce yourself."

"My mother . . ."

Cowell laughed. It was not a pleasant laugh. "No, don't worry. She isn't one of these," he said, gesturing behind him at the eleven robed figures. "She's part of my *other* flock." He winked. "My day job, as it were. Ministering to the sheep that worship the sheep god. What you see here is my *real* parish. This is the *real* church. Not those idiots to whom I minister the rest of the time. The irony is rather intoxicating, isn't it? I preach to your mother about the dangers implicit in the sin of sodomy, and we pray to sweet Jesus that the demon of homosexuality leaves you, but all the while I'm keeping track of her faggot son. Her same faggot son who sneaks around on summer nights on his bicycle far from home."

"I need your help," Mikey blurted out. "I've done something bad."

"What did you do, Mikey? What did you do that was 'bad'?"

"I cast a spell," he said, weeping. "All I wanted was for the guys who were beating me up to pay for what they did, and to stop. You guys know about this stuff. I've brought something to life and I need to send it back."

"Send it *back*? Why would you want to send it *back*? And to where? If you gave it life, it exists. It's here."

"It keeps on hurting people. This thing. It's all my fault. This isn't what I wanted. I need to send it back."

"Is that really the truth, though? You say you wanted them to pay. From what you say, it sounds like they're paying."

"What do you mean? I want it to stop!" Then the awareness came to him, coldly and inexorably.

All this time I thought I was alone. But I haven't really been alone, have I? Not since that night. Maybe even before.

"No, you haven't been alone." Dimly, Mikey realized that Cowell had read his thoughts and answered him with words. "For that matter, you're an intelligent boy. Haven't you asked yourself how you knew where to find us? You'd never been here before that night, had you?"

"I need you to help me!" he screamed. "I need you to send this thing *back*!"

Cowell sighed. "Mikey, you still don't understand, do you? We already did help you. You called out to us and we answered."

"*What?*"

"You found our website, didn't you? Or rather," Cowell added with saturnine humour, "*it* found *you*. Auburn is special, Mikey. Haven't you noticed? It has a very special history. I know you've heard the stories. I hadn't, till I moved here to start my . . . other church. These hills have been home to people like us for over one hundred years. There is tremendous power here. I found the coven soon after I moved to this perfect little town, with its pretty houses and shady streets. It didn't take me long to become the leader, either. I have . . . well . . . let's just say, a certain past of my own that made me a more natural and appropriate leader than any they'd found before."

"But why me? Why did you choose me?"

"You were drawn to us," Cowell said. "You saw us. You discovered our secret. You know what we can do. So we struck a bargain with you, one you could have never dreamed you were entering into. Everything has led to this moment. Even your grandmother's heart attack was a gift from us. If your parents had been home that night, you would never have had the courage to kill that poor cat, or cast that spell. So we sent them away. It's all led to tonight. You do know what tonight is, don't you, Mikey?"

"Halloween," Mikey said dumbly. "It's Halloween."

"Halloween, Samhain, All Hallows Eve . . . it has so many names. But it's a holy night. Especially tonight. Tonight the earth and the moon are perfectly aligned." Cowell seemed to notice Wroxy for the first time. He turned and bowed to her in a courtly fashion, then nodded to two of the robed men behind her. They seized Wroxy's arms and twisted them behind her back. "Isn't that how you explained it, little witch, with your cards and your crystals? Well, little witch?" For a moment, Cowell's eyes seemed to catch the sullen glare of the firelight, turning them red. "Shall I tell you what the lunar eclipse *really* means tonight, especially here in Auburn?"

Adrian stepped out of the fire, nude and unburnt. The skin of his glorious body shimmered in the reflected glow of the flames, golden and translucent. Mikey swam with familiar longing at the sight of him in spite of himself, in spite of everything.

Someone to love me, someone to hold me.

Mikey looked down. Adrian was floating. His feet hovered six inches above the ground.

Adrian's voice was soft, familiar. The voice of a lover, the voice of those long, secret hours in his bedroom after school. The voice from his dreams before that. "Hello, Mikey." He reached out to touch Mikey, who flinched and drew away. "I love you. Do you love me?"

Mikey shook his head wildly from side to side. "No! Go away! I don't love you! I hate you!"

Adrian began to change again. This time, the wide chest sank, becoming frail and crepuscular. The strong legs buckled and collapsed, becoming thin and weak, undefined and spindly. The thick blond hair darkened to brown, becoming thin and lank. The broad planes of Adrian's face narrowed, the skin becoming pale and dusted with acne above the cheekbones.

Mikey stared in horror. It was a face he knew well. His own.

"*I love you.*" The voice was mocking. A high, fluty voice that trembled, a voice often derided as effeminate. Mikey's own voice. "*Do you love me? Please love me! Please love me! Somebody love me!*"

Mikey turned away, feeling the familiar shame and revulsion for himself that he'd been taught was the normal and correct response to who he was. To *what* he was. To what he would always be.

Cowell sounded almost regretful. "You didn't understand the spell at all, did you? Didn't you understand what you were asking for?" Gently, he pulled Mikey's hands away from his face and looked into his eyes, like an earnest father who needed to impart wisdom to an errant son.

And suddenly Mikey *did* understand. His call had been answered after all. The demon he had summoned took its power from the realm of Mikey's own hatred and terror. His own hatred and terror had left his body when he cast the spell. Adrian was the incarnation of his own desire for revenge. The form Adrian had taken to seduce Mikey was Mikey's own idealized vision of beauty.

Adrian had watched Mikey's classmates torment him, and Adrian hated them. Adrian had watched Mikey's parents dismiss him and hold him in contempt, and Adrian hated them, too. Adrian lived inside him and always had. Adrian loved Mikey to death and would love him from world to world. Adrian had always been there, and always would be.

"You came here to stop him, didn't you?" Cowell said. "You wanted to send him back. All right, we'll help you. But we need something from you, too. Adrian told you, I believe, that his father was from here. Indeed he is. Auburn is his home, and always has been. Tonight is his homecoming. But Adrian's father can't just come through the doorway with only the blood of goats. Goats just whet his appetite."

"Adrian's father—"

"The true father of this world. He has so many names, and so many children. Adrian is only one of many."

"Oh, God, Mikey, get away from these people!" Wroxy thrashed against the bodies that held her. "Get the fuck away from them! Don't listen to them! Don't help them!"

"Take this knife," Cowell said. He offered Mikey the gleaming blade. Mikey shook his head. "You have a choice," Cowell continued. "Spells have to run their course. They always do. But if you want to send him away, you can. Just kill yourself. Be tonight's sacrifice. Bring Adrian's father home. Your blood will make this ancient soil richer, and Adrian will die with you, and the spell will return to the earth."

Cowell paused, idly testing the sharpness of the blade against his thumb. "Or else," he mused, "let Adrian live. No one will ever love you as much as Adrian does. Let him grow stronger. Be fair, after all. He'll kill and kill, and maybe you can learn to live with the guilt." Cowell watched Mikey's face, waiting for the words to sink in. "You already know real horror, Mikey. It isn't killing or demons. The only real horror is being alone. Don't you ever get tired of crying? One way or another, you can end it tonight."

Mikey felt a heavy, warm hand on his shoulder behind him. A strong arm slipped around his waist. "*I* love you," Adrian whispered into his ear. His white-blond hair shone in the firelight, and there was only tenderness in the bluest eyes Mikey had ever seen. Adrian was again the nineteen-year-old boy Mikey had first seen walk into his homeroom class and sit down next to him. "My love is eternal. I'll always protect you. And you'll never have to see my true shape again."

"Or," Cowell said, "there is a third choice. We need the sacrifice one way or another, and it had to come to this place of its own free will. One life or another, He doesn't care who opens the doorway." Without turning, he gestured behind him, toward Wroxy, with the knife. "We can make it so that no one ever finds out what happened to her, Mikey. You already know what we can do. You've seen how far our powers can reach, haven't you? Besides, Adrian can take the guilt away. That's a promise. And you and he will be together forever. No more guilt, no more pain. No more tears, ever. Doesn't that sound wonderful? All you have to do is kill her."

Wroxy's mouth opened in a perfect oval of horror. "No, Mikey," she whispered. "Oh, God, no. No, please don't. For the love of God, Mikey, I'm your best friend. Don't do it."

It was me, Wroxy thought wildly. *It was always me. The cards foretold this. I thought I was reading for Mikey, but they were about me. I am the Queen of Swords. I was the one being led by the malefic force, not Mikey. The moon is mine, not his. I am the betrayed friend. I am the sacrifice.*

"Change your life, Mikey," Adrian whispered. "Change theirs."

Mikey felt general love wash over him for the first time, a terrible yearning love that overrode all his fear. Love for Wroxy, love for Adrian, love for the town of Auburn and all the people in it he yearned to forgive. And yes, he was very tired of crying.

Above the earth the low red moon slipped completely into the penumbra and entered full eclipse. Mikey's eyes met Wroxy's and she saw his mouth form the words: *Forgive me.*

Then he swung the knife in a wide arc and plunged it very, very hard into Wroxy's chest.

Wroxy gasped in shock. There was no pain, merely enormous pressure at her sternum as the blood began to leak out around the seven-inch blade that protruded from her chest. She looked at Mikey through dying eyes, then her world went dark and her eyelids fluttered and closed.

Mikey caught her heavy body as it fell. He cradled her, rocking back and forth in his twisted, loving grief, weeping, knowing at the same time that this was the last time he would ever have to cry. Mikey held Wroxy close, not wanting to let go. He knew what was coming next.

In the air above them, a cloud bank began to form. Inside it, lightning flashed, and Mikey smelled the metallic tang of blood and sulfur.

Adrian ran his fingers through Mikey's hair and gently drew him to his feet. He led Mikey away from Wroxy's body, away from the circle of witches who had joined hands and begun to chant.

Passively Mikey allowed Adrian to guide him into the shadows outside the ring of firelight. Adrian turned Mikey around slowly and put his arms around Mikey's waist, pulling him close. Then Adrian kissed him. Mikey surrendered to the insistent pressure of Adrian's open mouth and felt himself drain away like water.

I would die for love. Yes, I would die for it.

I would kill for it.

Afterword: The Road Home to Auburn—On the Writing of *October*

If you want to know how *October* came about, you're going to have to bear with me for a bit. The story of how it happened is circuitous, and it starts in 1987. It's a writer's story. It's not in any way essential to understanding anything about Mikey, or Wroxy, or Auburn, or the witches, or even the era in which *October* is set, though all of those things come into play. You could skip it entirely and be none the poorer.

But if you're interested in how stories come out, specifically how this one came about, I'll tell you.

The world in which *October* is set—a pre-millennial, 1990s world of dial-up computers, pay phones, phone books, and bright yellow Sony Discmans—is very different from the world in which it is being read in the current edition from the CZPeBook imprint, which is being published in the autumn of 2017.

I wrote an early version of this story in late 2005 and early 2006 at the behest of novelist David Thomas Lord, who had struck a deal with a small LGBT publisher to develop a triad anthology of gay-themed Halloween novellas. The only other requisite theme was seasonal. In terms of story, we were entirely free to roam wherever we chose. There were to be no restrictions as to plot, character, or anything else, as long as the novellas encompassed some aspect of the gay experience in the horror realm, and were set during the Halloween season.

So I decided to go "home" with my novella, then titled *In October*.

In the summer of 1987, when I was twenty-five, my husband Brian and I sold our house in Toronto and moved to a small town fifty-seven kilometers west of Toronto called Milton. The move inadvertently set into motion an adventure that would have a life-changing effect on me as a writer, as well as give me a human gift that I never expected to receive.

Earlier that spring, Brian's mother, who lived in Guelph, farther west up the highway, had suffered a stroke. Her husband, Brian's father, was bereft. For a week, it was touch and go as to whether or not her condition would deteriorate. We were told that another stroke would likely kill her. Brian and I had checked into a hotel, spending the days with her at the hospital, or tending to his father's grief and terror at possibly losing the love of his life. At the end of the week, we were ragged—nerves worn to the nub, eyes red-rimmed from tears and lack of sleep.

And yet, miraculously, as the week progressed, she began to improve. She'd lost the ability to speak clearly, but her wryness and sense of humour had returned. We exhaled the emotional breath we felt we had been holding for five days and began to breathe again.

That afternoon we decided to take a leisurely drive back to Toronto this time, as opposed to rushing back home along the same highway we'd taken, in the opposite direction, that terrible night when the call had come through about her stroke. Travelling along back roads and smaller highways, we came to the town of Milton, a blip on the highway we'd passed dozens of times on the way from Toronto to Guelph.

As we drove down Martin Street, one of the town's main tributaries to Highway 401, we saw an Open House/For Sale sign in front of a stately red-brick Victorian, set back from the sidewalk on a glorious green lawn bordered with flowerbeds.

Partly because we were kicky from exhaustion, and partly because Brian and I love adventures, we decided to explore the house.

In Toronto we lived in a sleek townhouse in a trendy neighbourhood that embodied a particular type of 1980s-specific chic. I was young, newly married—in an era when gay marriage was not remotely part of the cultural language, nor was it possible to imagine that it ever would be—and was beginning to make a career for myself as a magazine writer while Brian established his medical practice.

And yet, in spite of all the reasons I should have loved our house, and the city in which we lived, it felt like it belonged in someone else's life, not mine.

The 1980s were all about hard edges and smooth, hyper-modern anodized surfaces. My persistent yearning was for corners, nooks, and cubbyholes. I craved patina, not gloss, and not only in houses. I craved it in people, and I craved it in my own life and work. In later years I would come to appreciate the detachment and paradoxical privacy that can come from living in a large city, but at twenty-five I craved a more intimate connection to a smaller, more immediate community.

Furthermore, Toronto was not my hometown: I had moved to the city in 1982 to attend college, and it's where I'd met Brian and started my professional life. Prior to that I had lived briefly in Paris, where I worked a fashion model after graduating from a boarding school outside a small city in western Canada, which was also not my home. My hometown, Ottawa, was a place where my family lived in between my father's diplomatic postings abroad, so while it was *technically* my hometown, it felt more like a beloved vacation destination of which I had fond memories.

And suddenly, stepping out of the car and inhaling the sweet scent of fresh-cut grass, lilacs, and spring earth from the farmer's fields beyond a town I had never visited before, I felt *at home* for the first time in my adult life.

The house was a restored 19th-century red-brick affair with a spacious living room, a stately, separate dining room, a family room with a studio above it. There were two bedrooms in the main wing, one of which I thought would make a splendid office. The house sat on a quarter acre of land, with a beautiful backyard full of flowers. Both of us felt an utter *coup de foudre* as we wandered through the house. The scent of the wood, warmed by the afternoon sun, was intoxicating.

Love is often illogical, and we were in the full throes of love with the house I had already begun thinking of as "our house." We put a conditional offer on it—for a fraction of what we had paid for our Toronto house—and the offer was promptly accepted. As soon as the Toronto house sold, which it did, quickly, the Milton property was ours.

In the next few years, I found the home I had been looking for during my young but nonetheless relentlessly peripatetic life.

That first year I set up my writing room in the loft that the previous owners had built as a quilting studio, but in spite of the high ceilings and impossibly perfect sunlight, I felt lost in the size of it and eventually installed myself in a small, cozy, book-lined room under the eaves at the top of the house.

The local newspaper, *The Canadian Champion*, took me on as a freelancer, allowing me to explore Milton and its people in the way I knew best—by talking to them, interviewing them, and writing about them.

I wrote a prize-winning feature profile of a local young police officer working the night shift in a small town. I followed the production of *Oklahoma!* at E.C. Drury High School over the course of several weeks leading up to the performances. I fell so deeply in love with the young actors and their work that I brought in a well-known fashion photographer from Toronto to shoot the portraits that accompanied the feature—an aspect of my process that was not appreciated by the photography department of the *Champion*.

I wrote about the town in any different way I could spin an angle, with the full support of my editor. In this age of diminished print media, it seems a surreal gift to have ever had that chance. My magazine career had continued to flourish and had become lucrative, but I never turned down the pittance the newspaper offered me for another chance to chronicle the life and times of my town.

Writing about the town led to connections, to friendships, to a sense of belonging. As a chronicler of small-town life, I had a role that was time-honoured and welcomed. More importantly, I was allowing myself to plot a literal personal geography, which would eventually form the basis of a literary geography.

In 1990, I read Anne Rice's *The Witching Hour*. As a reader, I was enthralled by the lushness of it, the rich historical detail, and the glorious descriptions, particularly of the Mayfair house in the Garden District of New Orleans. As a writer, I was intrigued to learn that Rice had used her own house as the model for the Mayfair house.

* * *

In the summer of 1992, at twenty-nine, I signed up for the summer session at Harvard to take two creative writing courses—one, a fairly conventional literary fiction course, the other a course in science fiction, fantasy, and horror, taught by the esteemed editor, critic, and anthologist, Kathryn Cramer. I would be thirty in September, and I needed some answers from myself about my intentions for my own future as a writer, the direction I wished my career to take, and how to make that happen.

I moved into Adams House for eight weeks with my word processor. On my second day there, I went to a local barber in Cambridge and asked him to give me as close a crop as he could without actually shaving my head. The gesture was symbolic as well as practical—the summer of 1992 in Cambridge was breathtakingly hot and humid, and if there was air-conditioning in the dorm, I barely noticed it.

The haircut also served the purpose of making me look nothing like myself. When I looked in the mirror, I saw a *tabula rasa*. The person in the glass had no history. He could be *anyone*. No one had ever told this person that he was a *wonderful* non-fiction writer and that he should probably work on that and leave fiction to the fiction writers—no one, frankly, including himself.

No one would say, "This is interesting, but we *know* you. This isn't *you*."

For eight weeks, the person in the mirror could reinvent himself and reimagine himself into any future he chose through sheer force of will and imagination, bringing everything he'd experienced to bear, including that precious newfound personal geography, and hopefully emerge as his own definition of a writer.

In Kathryn Cramer's class, exploring my version of the locational technique Anne Rice had employed in *The Witching Hour*, I wrote the first draft of a short horror story set in Milton, in our house on Martin Street.

The story, "Wild Things Live There," is about a young boy's terrifying encounter with an entity that disguises itself as an old woman named Mrs. Winfield, but which is, in actual fact, a member of a race of ageless, carnivorous trolls that make their homes wherever there are hills and caves. In the case of "Wild Things Live There," the rocky landscape is not only Milton itself, but also the Niagara Escarpment framing it.

In Cambridge, Massachusetts, five hundred miles away, the town and its people were vivid to me in a way that they never were when I was home.

The story would eventually be published in 1994 in *Northern Frights 3*, the third installment of Don Hutchison's World Fantasy Award-nominated anthology series of Canadian horror fiction.

By that time, Brian and I had left Milton and were again living in Toronto. The distance only served to sharpen and burnish the clarity of my memories of the time. Two more "Milton stories" were published in 1997: a werewolf story titled "Red Mischief" in *Northern Frights 4*, and a vampire story titled "The Dead of Winter" in *Brothers of the Night*, an anthology of gay vampire fiction I co-edited with Thomas S. Roche.

All three of these stories would be obliquely referred to in *In October* as part of the small town legends of the region.

By the time David Lord and I first talked about the novella anthology in 2005, I had already edited or co-edited four volumes of gay horror fiction myself, including two gay vampire anthologies with Thomas S. Roche. I'd also published a book of interviews with erotica writers on the topic of censorship, pornography, and popular culture, and a book of social and political essays. I was also the first-tier Canadian correspondent for *Fangoria*, and I had begun my tenure with *The Advocate*, the legendary LGBT news magazine for whom I would eventually write seven cover stories.

But during all that time, I hadn't written much fiction of my own, so the invitation to essay my first long-form fiction for this anthology was as flattering as it was daunting.

Still, the chance to bring together the disparate elements of my career and obsessions—horror fiction, social issues, and gay rights issues—was professionally irresistible. While one or two anthologies of gay "erotic horror" had been previously published, my anthologies *Queer Fear* and *Queer Fear 2* had been the first-ever pure gay horror fiction anthologies. Clive Barker hailed them as changing the face of horror fiction. We'd broken the ground, but I had participated in that groundbreaking as a curator, not as a storyteller.

With *In October*, I would finally be able to throw my hat in the ring. The genesis of the novella was, of course, bullying. Today it's recognized as the pernicious, destructive force that it is, but at the time I was growing up (and even into the 1990s, when the story is set) it was considered to be a rite of passage, particularly for boys. For gay boys, particularly femme gay boys, it was the price we paid for not being able to be anything but who we were.

During my first year in Milton, someone to whom I was not "out" had told me an off-the-cuff story about a gay man who had been beaten to a pulp outside one of the roadhouses on the outskirts of the town. Though possibly apocryphal, the story was delivered in such a deadpan, matter-of-fact tone that it chilled me. We lived across the street from a Catholic church that put up crosses on its lawn every Mother's Day in memory of "the babies murdered by abortion," and left the gruesome mock graveyard up until Father's Day. Milton was also the home of a rabidly homophobic preacher with political ambitions and a growing platform.

From the vantage point of thirty years, it seems surreal to imagine how easily we took for granted that this sort of ugliness could co-exist in a beautiful small town with so many genuinely kind and loving people in it, and that I could make a life there, but that was where the world was in 1987, even in Canada.

Another story I heard, this time from a group of teenagers at the Golden Griddle restaurant in the Milton Mall in 1989, detailed the apparent existence of some sort of coven of witches that had been spotted on occasion on the outskirts of town. I suspected this was a classic exurban legend, but I was entranced nonetheless. On the other hand, there was no serious talk of black magic or Satan worship, and in fact there was an absence of the sort of lurid detail that usually accompanies this sort of small-town story, which lent it some possible credence. In any case, I made a mental note and filed it away.

The town of Auburn, if it existed anywhere but in my imagination, would be geographically situated between Milton and the neighbouring town of Campbellville. I had first used Auburn in "Wild Things Live There," and had given it many of the attributes of Milton, with a few embellishments. All that was left, in the writing of *In October* was to bring them all together.

The eventual result was the story you just read, about Mikey and Wroxy, the witches of Auburn and, of course, Adrian. In Wroxy I celebrated the friendships that many gay boys have with edgy straight girls who are often outcasts themselves.

I was once asked, during the Q&A session after a public reading of this story, if I "hated" Milton, or if I regretted having lived in a small town as an adult gay man who could have lived anywhere else, and if that was the reason I set horror stories there. The question struck me as absurd, but I could see where someone blessed with an uncomplicated imagination could draw that conclusion.

In fact, I replied, the answer was quite the opposite.

I loved Milton. I loved living there, and I loved being a part of it in its last iteration as an authentic small Ontario town before the suburban creep turned it into just another bedroom community for Toronto.

These horror stories are love letters from a horror writer. The beauty of my former hometown is as lovingly rendered as I could manage within the limitations of my talent, and there are flashes, here and there, of people I've loved. Each of the stories is a grouping of mental photographs of a vanished time, carefully placed in an album of words. The novelist Jane Rule once wrote that she had one audience in mind when she wrote—herself, decades later.

In a way, I suppose, I've unconsciously followed Rule's lead with these stories, because they take me back to those years with a clarity that is personally shocking. And the people who populate these stories were, and are, as real to me as people I've actually known.

In the summer of 2017 I was approached by a young filmmaker from Los Angeles about the possibility of optioning *In October* as a feature. I was already a massive fan of his edgy, queer-themed short horror films, which were a marriage of technical filmmaking expertise, a brilliant, beautiful vision, and a sophisticated horror aesthetic that spoke to me from the first frame of the first film of his I'd seen.

His inquiry about *In October* surprised and delighted me.

The original anthology was long out of print, and seemed very much of its time. I was flattered that it had caught his attention. It had also always seemed to be the most unfilmable of all my books. Too, after a gruesome battle with the company charged with handling the post-mortem affairs of the original publisher, which was now out of business, the rights to *In October* had reverted to me in 2015.

I'd made vague plans to have *In October* anchor a collection of my short horror fiction at some point, but my publisher gently pointed out that, at more than fifty thousand words, the possibility of that anchor thematically sinking the entire ship was something worth considering. *In October*, for better or for worse, had always been a novel, not a novella.

Speaking to the young filmmaker, however, I was able to see that while *In October* was, in his words, "a bit dated," its central theme—the homicidal effects of bullying on LGBT children—was more relevant in 2017 than it had been when I wrote the story. The cultural discussion around bullying has reached an unprecedented level of mainstream currency. In addition, as a society we have moved past the binary "gay and lesbian" conversation to encompass an umbrella of variations on queerness that are now as likely to be reached for by many kids as they are by adults.

In a film of In October, *could Mikey be genderqueer?* he asked. *Could Wroxy perhaps be bi?*

My answer, which came with surprising relief on my part, was, *Yes, absolutely they could be.*

They could easily have been all those things in my original written version, and likely might have been if I had been writing *In October* today, for a 2017 audience, and if I'd had the nuanced language of queer culture available to me then that I do now. Every character written by a writer shares at least a trace of that writer's DNA, perhaps even that writer's history.

Wroxy and Mikey were no exception to that rule. In a way, they were as constrained by the sociopolitical nomenclature of the times in which they were written as they were by the fascist high school politics of the era, or the dictates of Mikey's mother's church, or the dark witchcraft he employs to exact his revenge in a Faustian bargain for safety and love that ultimately destroys both of them. We had words like "gay" and "lesbian" and "bisexual" and "transsexual." Words like "transgender" or "genderqueer" or "gender fluid," or even "queer"—in the modern LGBTQIA sense of the term it has now become—were still years off from being accessible to a mainstream audience.

And that's the one thing that would not have changed—the notion that a young person can be so broken by the cruelty of his or her tormentors, including their parents, that his or her moral core is ultimately shattered. I wonder about this every time I hear about violence perpetrated by an outcast teenager, or yet another tragic suicide. It's not about "weakness," as it's sometimes cruelly dismissed. It's about the notion that some good people can only bend so far before they snap.

After my conversation with the young filmmaker, I revised my ill-conceived plan of including *In October* in a future story collection. I approached my publisher, Sandra Kasturi, about releasing it as a standalone eBook from ChiZine Publications, retitled *October*.

Because technology is as capricious a mistress as the social mores that have changed more swiftly in the last decade and a half than they have at any other time in recent history, I found myself with an onerous task—since, as I've mentioned, the original publisher was out of business, and the manuscript of *In October* had been written on a floppy disk in an obsolete computer program (and I had absolutely no idea where the floppy disk was anyway) I decided to eschew scanning the actual book pages and retype the almost fifty-thousand-word manuscript from scratch, which my kind friends and colleagues stopped short of reminding me was a bit idiotic.

But I had my reasons.

In addition to minor revisions to the text and giving it that "one last pass" from a gifted editor that it never had in 2005, I wanted to re-inhabit the world of Mikey and Wroxy and Auburn myself, from the inside, and bring it back to life for me as vividly as it was when I first conceived it.

If nothing else, I dearly hope that the story, including the actions, reactions, and choices made by Mikey and Wroxy, and the people around them, serves as a reminder of the fact that whatever all our differences might be, they're trumped by the things we have in common—hope, dreams, terrors, a need to feel safe, a desire to love and be loved.

I'd like to think that the current "author-preferred edition" is not only the version I had always wanted for the story, but also a more accessible version that is more in line with my novels *Enter, Night* and *Wild Fell* which exist in a world where horror, like life, encompasses people of all genders and orientations.

You, the reader, will be the ultimate judge of how well I've succeeded.

David Thomas Lord, whose real name was John Sumakis, died in 2016.

In the years since our first professional contact, our friendship had grown into a mutually supportive, much-treasured one—a friend-ship with a writer, and a man, of profound kindness and generosity. In his final years he was wracked with pain, but even in the midst of the worst of it, he extended himself far beyond what would ever have been expected of someone in his condition, and he did so without complaint. One of the most tragic aspects of his passing was how many stories he had left to tell and how many books he had left to write. Our field is lessened by the absence of his voice. While I would much rather have him at the other end of the phone, or in my email in-box in the morning, I confess there is a profound sense of *rightness* in being able to add his name as a dedicatee to the current edition.

Aside from everything else, John Sumakis was, in every sense, the true godfather of *October*.

Michael Rowe
Toronto, Ontario
July 2017

About the Author

Michael Rowe as born in Ottawa, and has lived in Beirut, Havana, and Paris. He is the author of the novels *Enter, Night* (2011), *Wild Fell* (2013), and *October* (2019.) A French edition of *Wild Fell* was published by Editions Bragelonne in Paris in 2016. An award-winning journalist and essayist, he is also the author of the nonfiction books *Writing Below the Belt* (1995), *Looking For Brothers* (1999), and *Other Men's Sons* (2004.) He has won the Lambda Literary Award, the Queer Horror Award, and the Randy Shilts Award for Nonfiction. He has been a finalist for the National Magazine Award, the International Horror Guild Award, the Sunburst Award, and the Shirley Jackson Award. He was for 17 years the first-tier Canadian correspondent for the legendary horror film magazine *Fangoria*, which he credits as the best job he ever had. As the creator and editor of the anthologies *Queer Fear* (2000) and *Queer Fear 2* (2002), Clive Barker hailed him in as having "changed forever the shape of horror fiction forever." He lives in Toronto with his husband, Brian McDermid in a Victorian house near an ancient graveyard.